THE WORLD OF INSPECTOR LESTRADE

THE WORLD OF INSPECTOR LESTRADE

M. J. TROW

THISTLE
PUBLISHING

All Rights Reserved

Copyright © M. J. Trow 2019

This first edition published in 2019 by:

Thistle Publishing
36 Great Smith Street
London
SW1P 3BU

www.thistlepublishing.co.uk

*To Tali, who grew up with Inspector Lestrade;
thank you, with all my love, for your patience!*

Contents

Reviews for the Lestrade series. ix
Caveat lectorum - Let the Reader Beware!. . . . .
   From Police Constable to Political Correctness
Coca Cola with Maskelyne 3
The Sawdust Ring – 1879 7
   The Victorian Circus; Lord George Sanger; Disraeli;
   Gladstone; Howard Vincent; George, Duke of Cambridge.
The Sign of Nine – 1886 25
   The Police; the Yeomanry; Wilkie Collins; Borley Rectory.
The Ripper – 1888 41
   Jack the Ripper; the East End; Ripperology; Prostitution;
   Serial Killers; Sir Charles Warren; Charles Bradlaugh;
   Public Schools.
The Adventures – 1891 . . . .
   Tennyson; Alma-Tadema; Edward VII; General Booth;
   Oscar Wilde; Religion; Death; Spiritualism.
Brigade – 1893. 87
   Survivors of the Charge of the Light Brigade; Army;
   Workhouse; Country House Set; Goron of the Sûreté;
   the Kaiser; Gilbert and Sullivan; Henry Irving, Bram
   Stoker; Daisy Warwick
The Dead Man's Hand – 1895. 109
   London Underground; Empire; Marshall Hall; H.G.
   Wells; Aubrey Beardsley; W.G. Grace; Drunkenness
The Guardian Angel – 1898 123

Victoria's Small Wars; Garnet Wolseley; Lady Randolph Churchill; Cycling.
The Hallowed House – 1901 133
Politics; Churchill; Keir Hardie; Bonar Law; Suffragettes; Kipling.
The Gift of the Prince – 1903 149
Queen Victoria; Arthur of Connaught; Motoring.
The Mirror of Murder – 1906 159
Inventions; John Buchan
The Deadly Game – 1908. 165
Olympic Games; Scouting; Forensics; G.K. Chesterton; Journalism.
The Leviathan – 1910 179
Navy; Jackie Fisher; William Stead; Mata Hari; True Crime.
The Brother of Death – 1912/3 193
CID; Margaret Murray; Music Hall; Cleveland Street Scandal; Valentine and Samuel Baker; Fashion.
The Devil's Own – 1913. 215
Hangmen; Prisons; Communications; Money.
The Magpie – 1920. 227
First World War; Secret Services; Cinema; Michael Collins; G.B. Shaw; Vernon Kell; Basil Thompson.
The Kiss of Horus – 1923. 243
Archaeology; Flying; Roaring Twenties.
The Giant Rat of Sumatra – 1936 255
London Sewers; Charles Fort; Flying Squad.
The Amateur of 221B2 265
The Imposters: Actors who have played Lestrade (and lost!) 271
The Wit and Wisdom of Sholto Lestrade. 271

Reviews for the Lestrade Series

'This is Lestrade the intelligent, the intuitive bright light of law and order in a wicked Victorian world.'
Punch
'A wickedly funny treat.'
Stephen Walsh, *Oxford Times*
'...M.J. Trow proves emphatically that crime and comedy can mix.'
Val McDermid *Manchester Evening News*
'Good enough to make a grown man weep.'
Yorkshire Post
'Splendidly shaken cocktail of Victorian fact and fiction...Witty, literate and great fun.'
Marcel Berlins, *The Times*
'One of the funniest in a very funny series...lovely lunacy.'
Mike Ripley, *Daily Telegraph*
'High-spirited period rag with the Yard's despised flatfoot wiping the great Sherlock's eye...'
Christopher Wordsworth, *Observer*
'Barrowloads of nineteenth century history...If you like your humour chirpy, you'll find this sings.'
H.R.F Keating, *Daily Telegraph*
'Richly humorous, Lestrade has quickly become one of fiction's favourite detectives.'
Yorkshire Evening Post
'No one, no one at all, writes like Trow.'
Yorkshire Post

Caveat lectorum – Let the Reader Beware!

From Police Constable to Political Correctness

In 1891, the year in which *The Adventures of Inspector Lestrade* is set, Thomas Hardy had his *Tess of the d'Urbervilles* published in serial form by *The Graphic*, one of the country's leading magazines. The editor was not happy with certain scenes which he felt would upset Hardy's genteel readership. In one instance, when Angel Clare has to carry Tess over a minor flood, Hardy had to write in a handy wheelbarrow so that Tess and Angel had no bodily contact. When it came to Tess's seduction by the dastardly Alec d'Urberville, the pair go into a wood and a series of dots follows...

Even with all this whitewash, reviews of the revised version were mixed and it was many years before *some* of the Grundyisms* were restored to their original glory and *Tess of the D'Urbervilles* was established as another masterpiece of one of Britain's greatest writers.

In the *Lestrade* series, I hope I have not offended anyone, but the job of an historical novelist – and of an historian – is to try to portray an accurate impression of the time, not

---

* From Mrs Grundy, a priggish character in Thomas Morton's play *Speed the Plough*, 1798.

some politically correct Utopian idyll which is not only fake news, but which bores the pants off the reader. Politicians routinely apologize for the past – historical novelists don't. we have different views from the Victorians, who in turn had different views from the Jacobeans, who in turn…you get the point. When the eighteenth century playwright/actor Colley Cibber rewrote Shakespeare – for example, giving *King Lear* a happy ending! – no doubt he thought he was doing the right thing. He wasn't.

That said, I don't think that a reader today will find much that is offensive in the *Lestrade* series. So, read on and enjoy.

COCA-COLA WITH MASKELYNE

Coca-Cola began life as a painkiller, developed by John Pemberton, a Confederate colonel, who became a morphine addict after suffering wounds in the civil war. He registered his French Wine Coca nerve tonic in 1885. It could, he claimed, cure morphine addiction, nervous disorders various, headaches, indigestion and impotence. It did not become popular in Britain until after the Second World War but technically, it was available by the time Sholto Lestrade was an Inspector.

Nevil Maskelyne was born nine years after Lestrade, the son of a stage magician and became the most famous prestidigitator of his generation.

SPOILER ALERT; Lestrade never met Maskelyne and he never knowingly drank Coca-Cola. His old oppo, Fred Wensley *did* (see *The Kiss of Horus*) but Lestrade understood it was something to sprinkle on fish and chips. Even so...

...Back in the mists of time – 1983 to be exact – my good lady wife (a voracious reader, Gentle Reader) said, 'I have nothing to read.' At the time, the BBC was showing (again!) the Basil Rathbone Sherlock Holmes films. Basil was far and away the best Sherlock we've had, but I found the whole premise preposterous. He would say things like, 'There's an East Wind blowing, Watson,' (quoting, I fear, Arthur Conan Doyle) and Watson, played by Nigel Bruce, would mutter something incomprehensible and look confused. Immediately I realized that someone like Holmes – irascible, egocentric and a junkie – would not tolerate Watson's imbecility for a moment. Into this scenario stumbled a tall actor – whose name I can rarely remember but on looking on IMDb I discover is Dennis Hoey – playing Inspector Lestrade. He would take off his regulation bowler and beg Holmes for his help. 'We're so useless down at the Yard, Mr 'Olmes, that we've come to pick your gargantuan brain to 'elp us with our henquiries' – or words to that effect. I found this ludicrous, so I turned the tables. In the book that I wrote for my wife (*The Adventures of Inspector Lestrade* originally called *1891*) Lestrade is the crime-solver, albeit accident-prone, a little gauche and not always *precisely* right in his deductions – and Holmes and Watson are merely annoying amateurs who sometimes get in Lestrade's way.

My wife lovingly typed out the ms – I wrote longhand and I am still doing so today – and we sent it to publishers various. 'Alas,' said one rejection slip, 'only a 7½% solution, I fear' (again quoting Conan Doyle) and it turned me down. I had no agent and not much clue in those days – in fact (don't hate me!) I didn't even know who the murderer was until halfway through the book. But, on the seventh try, I struck lucky and Hilary Hale (nee Watson – no relation) of Macmillan agreed to publish *if I got my history right.*

As an historian, I was seething, so I rang up and complained.

'You've got Baden Powell in the book,' Hilary said.

'Yes,' I said. 'Is that a problem?'

'For the whole of 1891, Baden Powell was in Malta. You've got him in Ireland.'

Realization dawned. The electric light bulb moment. Even in fiction, if it's historical fiction, you've got to get your facts right. So I altered it and the rest is history.

Even so, I cheat. Historical fiction is immensely popular today but it is actually quite difficult to write. Having William the Conqueror saying, 'Hi y'all,' wouldn't impress anybody. Alternatively, neither would the eleventh century Norman French he would actually have spoken. A writer has to find a middle way and I hope, with the Lestrade series, I have. '"Thanks, Sue," he said' is a pretty conventional line in any novel at any time, but actually it is a quotation from Thomas Hardy (*Jude the Obscure*) in 1894. Throughout the series, I used phrases that were current as I wrote. So Sherlock Holmes himself was prone to say 'Have a nice day' when those ghastly words were on the lips of every supermarket checkout person in the land. All Lestrade's rookies have the names of retail outlets still going for years after his time – Dickens and Jones, Bang and Olufsen, Bourne and Hollingsworth, even Guest, Keen and Nettlefold. I deliberately tease my readers with people and situations that *could* be real, but actually aren't, or are taken from a different time. For instance, most of the hauntings at Borley Rectory (qv) happened well after Lestrade's time, but I place them in 1886 (in *The Sign of Nine*). Likewise, Dr Margaret Murray's work on witchcraft was written years after she appears in a Lestrade story (*The Brother of Death*). There is no evidence that the IRA leader Michael Collins (qv) had access to vast funds of the type referred to in *The Magpie*; and still less that the Grand Duchess Anastasia escaped to England after the slaughter of her family. In fact, *au contraire*, as Goron of the Sureté would have said, since I wrote that book, remains believed to be hers have been found in the Koptiaki woods near Ekaterinburg in the Urals.

Several people have asked me where the name of the East End ganglord Chubb Rupasobly came from. Wearing my other hat as a military historian, I wrote a book some years ago called *The Pocket Hercules* about William Morris who led the 17th Lancers at Balaclava. I obtained copies of letters written from the Crimea which had been deciphered by the secretary of one of Morris's descendants. Wrestling with Victorian handwriting (going in two directions to save paper on campaign) is not easy and the best the brave lady could do with one signature was 'Chubb Rupasobly'. Actually, it was Morris's brother officer, John Reynolds!

And sometimes, I just plain get it wrong. For *The Dead Man's Hand* I spent three hours in the London Transport Museum in Covent Garden, learning how to drive a virtual 1890s Tube train. I bought several books (in those pre-Internet days) and thoroughly – as I thought – immersed myself in the railwayana of the time. But – be warned, Gentle Writer – there is always someone out there who knows more than you do. I wrote the book, had it published and, months later, received a 'fan' letter.

'Dear Mr Trow,
  'I thoroughly enjoyed *Lestrade and the Dead Man's Hand*, but you *do* realise that in 1895, there *was* no 9.38 from Penge.'

The following presents the *chronological* story of Lestrade's life. It is not actually in the order in which the books were written.

THE SAWDUST RING

1879
'In the circus, nothing is what it seems...'

*W*alk up! Walk up! This way for the greatest show on earth! It is 1879. Disraeli is at Number Ten. The Zulu are being perfectly beastly to Lord Chelmsford. And Captain Boycott is having his old trouble again.

What has this to do with the young Detective-Sergeant Sholto Lestrade? Absolutely nothing. Or has it? He has his work cut out investigating mysterious goings-on at 'Lord' George Sanger's Circus. First, the best juggler in Europe is shot in full view of a thousand people. Then Huge Hughie, the dwarf, dies an agonizing death under the Ether Trick. Finally, the Great Bolus dies by swallowing the wrong sword. And all of this after two bodies have been found with multiple slashes...

And what is the link with Mr Howard Vincent, founder of the CID? And has the Prince Imperial really been caught by the Impis? A trail of murder is laid among the llama droppings as the World's Second Greatest Detective goes undercover to solve the Case of the Sawdust Ring.

'Good roads, good times and merry tenting' – The Victorian Circus

The circus began as a fixed entertainment in ancient Rome. Major cities had their own circuses – the Circus Maximus in Rome itself was the best known – which were horse-racing and charioteering circuits that commanded the sort of money, relatively, that F1 does today.

London's largest theatres in the eighteenth century had circus acts, especially clowns, bareback horse riding and high-wire trapeze acts. That was fine for the London crowds, but the provinces had nothing similar, so a handful of men took to the roads to bring entertainment to the people. It could be a make or break experience financially. Abraham Saunders and Pablo Fanque died broke; George Sanger became a millionaire.

Philip Astley was the first circus impresario, travelling to Dublin in 1773 and performing in an open-air ring. The system was called tenting and it drew crowds from all classes who queued up just to watch the heavy, horse-drawn wagons rumble past. Long before animal rights became an issue, the Victorians were fascinated to see elephants, lions, tigers, sealions and other menagerie performing 'before their very eyes'. The parade was an integral part of all this with gilded carriages, plumed horses and bespangled acrobats.

Military bands blasted the circus's arrival and the lions in their cages roared on cue. Pauline de Vere, the lion queen of Bostock's, often dressed up as Britannia with her favourite lion, Nero, at her feet, together with a lamb – the Victorians were heavily into their Biblical and classical imagery.

'Walk up! Walk up!' the clown on stilts roared as he welcomed the punters – 'Roll up!' came much later. The smaller circuses performed in the open air with a rope around the stage. The larger ones had huge tents – the big top rose like a giant mushroom with yards of canvas and miles of rope. Strongmen, tent-hands, clowns, *everybody* heaved that tent into position and anchored it with pegs and guy ropes. For evening shows, candles and flares lit the way and the ring itself. George Sanger was the first impresario in the world to exhibit on three stages, later immortalised by Barnum and Bailey and the Ringling Brothers.

Aerial acrobatics were hugely popular. Often performing without a safety net, men and women in tights and spangles swung through the air – the daring young man on the flying trapeze was not just a Music Hall song. Leotard was gyrating at London's Alhambra Theatre by 1861, giving his name to a vest. Blondin was walking British tightropes long before he crossed the Niagara Falls.

Science came to the aid of the performers. Volta electrified himself and lit gas jets with his fingertips. He also set fire to handkerchiefs, often donated by his audience. Miss Victorina swallowed a light bulb that shone through her flesh. Sword-swallowers were slightly old hat until a member of her troupe developed a routine of bayonet swallowing, while said bayonet was fixed to a loaded rifle.

The high tension of these moments was broken by the antics of clowns. Long before we invented coulrophobia – fear of clowns – people loved them. It was mime and slapstick, developed from the *Comedia del Arte* of the seventeenth century. Grimaldi was the stereotype, in his harlequin costume, taunting the audience and throwing buckets of confetti at them. The two best known were Thomas Lawrence and James Frowde, who began as performers associated with other acts, e.g. 'clown to the rope', 'clown to the horse' and so on.

But it was the animal acts that people paid to see. The Victorians were gushingly sentimental, especially when it came to children, deathbed scenes and animals. It is no accident that the Royal Society for the Prevention of Cruelty to Animals was set up in 1824 (under, as the name implies, royal patronage) whereas the National Society for the Prevention of Cruelty to Children (note, no royalty) did not see the light of day until sixty years later. For a pet-loving nation, the British were perfectly happy to pay good money to see lions, tigers, elephants, sealions, horses and other beasts performing to the whims of their trainers. This is because they had no idea how barbaric the training and conditions were and because they took horses, in particular, for granted as everyday objects. Elephants did 'handstands' on champagne bottles; bareback equestrians somersaulted from horse to horse; every other nag could say 'Yes' and 'No' and count to ten long before Roy Rogers' Trigger got in on the act in the 1950s. Bears made great dancers. So did lions, especially when the Lion King, Isaac Van Ambrugh, had a go at them. Ambrugh was making £300 a week at Astley's in 1838, and so impressed polite society that the great artist, Edwin Landseer, painted him snoozing in a cage with his big cats. He regularly put his arm or head inside a lion's mouth (as you do) to the delighted horror of the crowd.

Not everybody loved the circus. Sabbatarians opposed it because shows were held on Sundays; and a small, but increasingly vocal, group of what today would be called animal activists, referred to the circus as 'travelling death'. Ambrugh routinely starved his lions to make them more ferocious and beat them with iron bars.

The aspect of the Victorian circus which we would find the most repellent were the freaks. People with physical abnormalities or bizarre skills appeared in fixed shows called the penny gaffes in many British towns. Others travelled the roads. By the 1890s some of them were earning up to £20 a week. Glib showmen with all the patter revealed, for a price and beyond arm's length, the living mermaid, Siamese twins, midgets, giants and bearded ladies. Princess Lottie was twenty inches tall and weighed nine pounds. Prince Midge was half an inch taller and a pound heavier. Miss Rosina had no hands but crocheted superbly with her feet and painted with the brush in her mouth. Babil, the Giant Amazon stood nine feet tall in her plumed headdress. Every exhibit had an exotic story, designed to tug at the heartstrings rather than to repel. The Victorians loved it all. Today, all we have is *Britain's Got Talent* – it just isn't quite the same.

'LORD' GEORGE SANGER

Sanger had no actual title, but there is no doubt that he was circus royalty. He was born just before Christmas 1825, probably in Newbury (market day, Thursday), Berks. His dad had been a sailor who entertained his oppos on board ship with conjuring tricks and sleight of hand. When he left the navy, he and George's mum, Sarah, took to the roads with a peep show – calm down, dear, it didn't mean then what it does now. (See **The Circus**)

Little George started as an animal trainer – nothing too dangerous at first – canaries, mice, rabbits. They fired little cannons and walked tightropes (I'm not making this up, you know!). Local villagers, in what was still a superstitious age, accused him of witchcraft.

A snappy dresser, George became known as 'Gentleman George' and 'His Lordship' and won the heart of Ellen Chapman at the Stepney Fair in 1848. She became Madame Pauline de Vere, the Lion Queen of Bostock's Circus and married George in 1850. A year later, they were on the road with George's brothers, a Welsh pony and a tame oyster (I kid you not).

In 1871, the Sangers bought Astley's Amphitheatre, an eighteenth century entertainment centre in Lambeth, which wowed the crowd with equestrian daredevilry and trapeze work. It cost £11,000 at the time (around £1m today) and was still going strong twenty-eight years later.

Editor's note: Although George Sanger features in only one Lestrade story, set in 1879, we have to record the bizarre fact that he later became a murder victim himself. A disgruntled employee, Herbert Cooper, hacked him to death with an axe in 1911.

'Dizzy'

I have huge respect for Benjamin Disraeli, if only because he speaks the first word in the entire Lestrade series. That word is 'Gone?' and he is so pleased with it that he says it again – 'Gone?'

It's strangely monosyllabic for Dizzy, who was, to quote his arch-rival William Gladstone (qv) 'the arch-seducer' – but that is another story! There is no doubt that he had a way with words, however. There are more quotes from him in the average Dictionary of Quotations than anybody except Shakespeare (and we all know what a phrase-dropper he was).

He was born Benjamin D'Israeli (the apostrophe later disappeared as it has from most English words today) in 1804. His father was Isaac, and the man owned a huge library. Young Ben (constantly being referred to as a 'naughty boy' by the satirical magazine *Punch*) soaked up gallons of English history and attended various terrible schools in Walthamstow and Blackheath. These were 'crammers' where people were force-fed knowledge for knowledge's sake. One later alumnus of the Blackheath School was Sholto Joseph Lestrade, but that is another seventeen stories.

The trouble with Dizzy is that he didn't know what he wanted to be when he grew up. He became articled to a solicitor, then a barrister at Lincoln's Inn, wrote for a newspaper that lasted less than a year and then turned to romantic fiction – according to Gladstone, he never left it. The first book was called *Fifty Shades of Vivian Gray* (not really!) and it made Dizzy the talk of London town. On the proceeds, he went on the Grand Tour. This was a chaotic ramble around Europe (the equivalent of today's gap year) in which, pretending to soak up Classical culture, young men sowed wild oats in various brothels and bars before returning home to a life of sobriety and duty. Athens, Rome, Florence, Paris and Venice were on the itinerary, but because this was Dizzy and he was conscious of his Jewish heritage, he visited Jerusalem and Cairo too.

He came back prefiguring the Punk era of the 1970s, with chains all over his clothes and that tell-tale kiss-curl plastered to his head with Macassar oil. He tried seven times to get into parliament, not much bothered which party he served and finally made it (for Maidstone) in the year of Queen Victoria's (qv) succession, 1837.

Dizzy's maiden speech was a disaster and he was howled down in the Commons. Famously, he ended it with, 'Aye and though I sit down now, the time will come when you will hear me.' He got that right! He married a rich widow, Mrs Wyndham Lewis, and cadged £35k – depending on the money value tool you use, this could be the equivalent of as much as £50 million in today's money – to buy a country estate at Hughenden, Buckinghamshire. Nothing if not ambitious, Dizzy became head of the 'Young England' movement in the 1840s, a right-wing group of Tories who found Prime Minister Robert Peel's concept of country before party completely out of left field. He savaged Peel in the Corn Law debates of 1846, largely because Peel had already refused to give the man a cabinet post. When asked why he didn't destroy Disraeli by making this fact public, Peel said, 'I never wrestle with a chimney sweep.'

Under Lord Derby, Dizzy was the worst Chancellor of the Exchequer of the entire century; his sums didn't add up. By 1867, however, he had become a fluent debater and a consummate politician. Pinching ideas from Gladstone's Liberals, he bought in the Second Reform Bill, the 'leap in the dark' which doubled the electorate and gave the vote to the working class urban male (or men about town, as they were known).

He was Prime Minister twice, the second time from 1874-79 when he carried out a series of reforms that stabilized the country and established flag-waving imperialism as the way to go. 'Old Clo' as he was known behind his back after the street cry of the old Jewish rag-traders, bought half the Suez Canal with his old mate, Lionel de Rothschild, made the Queen, God bless her, Empress of India and sorted out Russia at the Congress of Berlin.

He had a nauseating relationship with the Queen, smarming around her with phrases like 'We authors, Ma'am' and explaining politics to her in words of one syllable. She loved flattery 'and when it comes to royalty, you should lay it on with a trowel'. By 1879, however, the year of the *Sawdust Ring*, Dizzy was on his way out for good.

'GLAD EYE'

'He treats me as if I were a public meeting,' Victoria famously said of Gladstone. The dear old queen was none too bright (which is why Disraeli spoke to her slowly and loudly) but 'Glad Eye' simply didn't have the basic vocabulary or the smarmy inclination to make that work. Not unreasonably, he expected the monarch to know what she was doing.*

William Ewart Gladstone was born in Liverpool in 1809, the son of a merchant. Astonishingly, we have the old boy on wax cylinder, so we know how he sounded as an old man; the vowels are pure Lowland Scots. For a man who lived all his life south of the border, Gladstone's accent sounds a little contrived; he was what today we would call a professional Scotsman. (In the nineteenth century, most English people, even Scotland-loving Queen Victoria, called them Scotch.)

Unlike Disraeli, who never quite flicked the chip off his shoulder, Gladstone went to public school – Eton, where he was only flogged once – and Christ Church, Oxford. A whizzo debater as President of the Oxford Union – 'inebriated,' as Disraeli said, 'with the exuberance of his own

---

* Victoria has recently been included in the Top Fifteen Most Influential Women Who Have Changed the World (a BBC poll). Why?

verbosity' – he couldn't decide on a career in politics or the church. His 1834 book *On Church and State* won the J K Rowling prize (just joking!) for The Most Boring Book Ever Written. As one of Robert Peel's Tories (returned for Newark) he was extremely right wing. In fact, the only reformist thing he really backed was the abolition of child labour in the coal mines and factories.

By 1841 he was President of the Board of Trade and became a supporter of Peel's Free Trade ideas. Even so, religion and morality, the twin supporters of his rigid Presbyterian upbringing, never quite disappeared and he resigned when Peel gave a cash grant to the Irish Catholic College at Mayrooth.

He and Mrs Gladstone (Catherine Glynn) lived at Hawarden Castle in Flintshire, North Wales, where he translated Homer and chopped down trees in his spare time. Unlike Disraeli, he had enormous physical stamina, which possibly explains his umpteen children and the fact that, once he was Prime Minister, he would nip out from Number Ten to save fallen women. Having 'saved' them, he would then whip himself to atone to God for his bestial fireside chats with them. Sigmund Freud would have had a field day.

Impressive in any political posts he held, he became Leader of the new Liberal Party after Lord Palmerston's death in 1865 and brought in a radical Reform Bill which failed.

Prime Minister by 1868, Glad Eye brought in the most dynamic ministry of the century. If something stood still, it was reformed. The buying of commissions in the army went. The Ballot Act made voting secret. Gladstone did his level best to pacify Ireland (Dizzy didn't have an Irish policy) by giving new rights to tenants. He scrapped the Irish (Anglican) Church. He outraged decent drinkers everywhere with his Licensing Act and in 1874, the new voters turned against him. 'We have been borne down,' he said, 'in a torrent of gin and beer.' And he was out, having to make way for Disraeli.

You can't keep an old religious maniac down, however, and the Bulgarian Atrocities of 1876 brought the soon-to-be-called Grand Old Man out of retirement. Hence his appearance in *The Sawdust Ring*.

HOWARD VINCENT (AND IGGY)

Charles Edward Howard Vincent, to give him his full monicker, was the son of a prebendary (well, somebody has to do it) born in 1849. Educated, up to a point, at Westminster, he went on to Sandhurst and bought a commission in the Royal Welsh Fusiliers in 1868. He studied military organisation in Russia, which can't have taken him very long, and wrote *Elementary Military Geography*, which was shortlisted for the Whitbread (joking, again), in 1872.

Having left the army, he entered the Inner Temple (you just turn right off Fleet Street) and was called to the bar (Wig and Pen Club) in 1876. At the same time, he was Lieutenant-Colonel of the Central London Rangers, which is not a euphemism for Ladies of the Night, no matter what you may have heard.

1877 saw the Trial of the Detectives (see **Watching the Detectives**) in which a number of quite senior coppers at the Yard got their come-uppance over a bribery scandal. Vincent had been to Paris to study police procedures there – at least, that was his story and he stuck to it. He wrote a report, with eighteen drafts, no less, and sent it to the Home Office.

Nobody seemed to notice that his idea for a shake-up at the Yard was a) based on the French *Sureté*, always dodgy and b) put said Howard Vincent in charge. The Home Office loved it – you have to understand that Home Secretaries in those days weren't of the highest intellectual calibre – and the system became the Criminal Investigation Department with dear old Howard at the helm.

His position was peculiar, but I won't dwell on that in a family book. He had the *status* of Assistant Commissioner, but the real Commissioner (Sir Edward Henderson) was not his boss. Neither could he actually give orders to his officers, because he was not part of the Force nor a magistrate (with me so far?). He increased plain clothed detectives' pay immediately, which mightily miffed the boys in blue, used the gentlemen of the Press to highlight cases to an alarming degree, dropped some of the physical requirements for detectives and tried to recruit the sons of gentry to up the intellectual level of the Met. This was a flop.

In brighter news, Vincent improved the quality of the *Police Gazette* which previously had been hanging on hooks in various coppers' outside privies, and set up the Convict Supervision Office, a rogues' gallery, complete with photos.

Did he really have a pet iguana? You'll have to read the book to find out.

GEORGE, DUKE OF CAMBRIDGE

He had the poppy eyes and elephantine girth of his cousin, the Queen. And was probably nowhere near as bright. George William Frederick Charles of the House of Hanover was born in Cambridge House (what an extraordinary coincidence), Hanover, Germany. The same age as the Queen, he was educated in Hanover until 1830, then privately in Britain. In the year of his cousin's coronation, he became a Brevet-Colonel (a sort of sideways, ex-officio rank) in the British army. He did a stint in Gibraltar for a year, then whizzed through a series of regiments – the 12th Lancers, the 8th Light Dragoons and the 17th Lancers – by 1842.

He must have got a great tan in the Ionian Islands for the next three years and was a Major-General by the age of twenty-six. This, he assured everybody, had nothing to do with whose cousin he was! He became Duke of Cambridge, Earl of Tipperary and Baron Culloden in July 1850. He was Inspector of Cavalry two years later and commanded the 1st Division (Guards and Highlanders) in the Crimea. Most brief bios say he was 'present' at the battles of the Alma, Balaclava and Inkerman and that says it all, really. His slowness at getting his Division moving on 25 October 1854 contributed significantly to the loss of the Light Brigade.

Commander-in-Chief and Field Marshal by 1862, Cambridge was a complete pain in the arse. A military dodo, he promoted men because of their family connections, not their ability – 'There is a time for everything,' he once said, 'and the time for change is when you can no longer help it.' On the other hand, he did improve the Staff College and set up annual war games to simulate real battlefield conditions. He lessened the use of the cat o' nine tails on law-breaking soldiers.

His basic problem was that he was C-in-C for far too long and the army paid the price for his old-fashioned stubbornness. If you are royalty, of course and you wait around for long enough, you get loaded with honours. He was colonel of eleven regiments, had more letters after his name than there are in the alphabet and the weight of the decorations on his chest must have been crippling. The universities of Oxford, Cambridge and Dublin were silly enough to give him Honorary degrees as a Doctor of Law.

The Sign of Nine

1886
'Hello, hello, hello...'
'Hello, hello, hello...'
'Hello, hello, hello...'

*I*t was a puzzle that faced Scotland Yard from its very beginning – whose was the limbless body found among the foundations? And in the murderous world of Sholto Lestrade, one question is invariably followed by another – what do a lecherous rector, a devious speculator and a plagiaristic novelist have in common? Answer: they're all dead, each of them with a bloody space where his skull used to be. And six others are to join them before our intrepid inspector brings the perpetrator to book.

But 1886 was a bad year for the Metropolitan Police. The People of the Abyss have heard the whisper and the spectre of Communism haunts the land. There is a new Commissioner, a regular martinet, at the Yard. And then, there is that very odd couple, sometime of Baker Street...

Lestrade braves haunted houses, machine-gun bullets and two Home Secretaries in his headlong hunt for the truth. And at last, this is the book that chronicles his now legendary impersonation of the Great Sarah Bernhardt. The Police Revue was never the same again.

THE THIN BLUE LINE

By the time Sholto Lestrade was born (1854) the idea of a regular police force was fully established in England and Wales. From the earlier Constables of the Watch and the Wakemen who patrolled town streets and warned communities of imminent danger, of fire, invasion and riot, emerged the county constabularies and their city equivalents.

They were all based on the Metropolitan Police established by the Home Secretary, Robert Peel, in 1829. We shall look in detail at the 'bad lot', as Arthur Conan Doyle called them, later, but their structure and training was followed by every other police force in the country.

The 'Hungry Forties', a decade of poverty and violence, had forced local authorities to up their game in terms of law and order. Chartism and the Irish potato famine combined to create dangerous mobs of starving men swarming over the countryside, looking for work, food, the vote and annual parliaments. Counties and municipal boroughs rushed to recruit suitable men for 'a police' to control all this, but the arrangements were haphazard and inconsistent. It was the usual Victorian problem – reform cost money and why should the haves continually pay for the have-nots? By 1853 only half the counties had implemented the Municipal Corporation Act which gave them the right to set up a force. Statistically, there was one copper to 1,000 people in the towns; one to 1,200 in the countryside – what crime epidemic?

The county forces were headed by the Chief Constable, invariably a local nob whose family owned half the land in the area. Central to the 'County Set', such men were also pillars of the church, rode to hounds and were the greatest and best of the great and good. Most of them had no idea of policing at all. Under them came superintendents, inspectors, sergeants and constables. Only the sergeant rank came from the army complete with three chevrons on the tunic sleeve, in a deliberate attempt to distance the police from the armed forces. Throughout the existence of the British army, it had been used by governments from time to time to 'aid the civil power' (see **Aiding the Civil Power**) and had a bad reputation among the working class. Most infamously, the Manchester and Salford Yeomanry and the 15th Hussars attacked an unarmed crowd at St Peter's Fields, Manchester in 1819. The result, with eleven dead and over 400 injured, came to be known as the Peterloo Massacre; the 15th had charged at Waterloo four years earlier.

So, in creating the Metropolitan Police, Peel had chosen non-military ranks and avoided the scarlet uniforms of the infantry. Unfortunately, he chose dark blue, the colour of the Light Cavalry; by coincidence, worn by both the MSY and the 15th at Peterloo. To make matters worse, by the 1860s, the tall stove-pipe hat and swallowtail tunic (essentially a civilian look) had been replaced by the 'Roman' helmet and high-collared tunic. Photographs of senior officers and constables from the 1880s and '90s show them to be indistinguishable in some senses from the army.

Development of the police forces was very slow. The nineteenth century saw a whirlwind of change, in technology, politics, education, industry and virtually everything else. Not so with the police. In theory, a man was still liable to serve as a parish constable, or find a substitute, until 1964!

What sort of police force did the country want? 'Aren't our policemen wonderful?' was not a phrase heard very often in Victorian England. When an officer was killed in the line of duty in 1833, the jury returned a verdict of justifiable homicide – the copper should not have interfered and had brought his death on himself. 'There's never one around when you need one' was far more common, if only because of the fixed point system of patrol whereby a constable was not allowed to leave a particular position, whatever the emergency. Polite society expected the police to be unobtrusive and deferential, which is why Inspector Jonathan Whicher got nowhere in the Road case of 1864. He knew perfectly well that Constance Kent had killed her brother, but her snobby, upper-class family refused to co-operate and most of the important people of the time agreed with them. The notion of the public-school educated toff detective (with or without a title) is the creation of the 1920s and '30s crime fiction writers.

The average recruit who joined the police was 26 years old and five foot eight inches tall. He had to be able to read, write and carry out basic arithmetic. He often came from a rural background. Peel encouraged men like this for the Met because they were strong, fitter than the average tubercular city dweller and less prone (it was hoped) to bribe-taking. The job brought warm clothing, the chance of promotion and steady pay; even a small pension. They didn't always live up to expectations. Of 214 men sworn in as constables in Liverpool in 1850, 65 had gone in the first twelve weeks and 112 after three years. The usual reason was drunkenness.

The men of the Liverpool force were typical in their daily routines. The section houses built for single men had reading rooms, mess rooms and smoking rooms. There was meat every day (a real luxury in the 1850s) and coal fires in the winter. The pay was regular. As the Chief Constable said to his recruits in 1852 (the same speech was made by his successor in 1879) – 'If you marry (and I hope you all will, if she is a good washer and can mend and darn) it is a nice thing to have plenty to begin house with.'

That said, a policeman's wages were those of an agricultural labourer and they didn't increase for years – hence the police strike of 1919. The average copper worked a seven day week, each shift lasting for up to seven hours. Rest days were rare. Most of the time, a copper walked his beat (a series of streets) in all weathers, day and night. He carried a hardwood truncheon for defence and a lantern for night work. These 'bulls' eyes' had convex lenses around a wick to throw light in all directions. Until the 1880s he carried a wooden rattle to summon the aid of a colleague who would be patrolling *his* beat some yards away. In that decade, a whistle was issued instead – the 'Metropolitan' make turns up regularly in antique shops today. The speed of patrol was 2½ miles an hour, the constables leaving the station in pairs until they peeled off to their own beat. They tramped about fourteen miles a day and were checked on regularly by beat sergeants.

Discipline was harsh. Coppers were not allowed into pubs (yeah, right!) nor to flirt with girls nor engage in any activity which might be construed as unbecoming. They couldn't even eat in public! Infringement of the rules would mean loss of pay, demotion or dismissal depending on the 'crime'.

The police developed their own jargon and speech patterns. 'I was proceeding in an easterly direction'; 'I had reason to believe'; 'in the pursuance of my enquiries'; 'acting on information received' were all current, even if 'Mind 'ow you go' and 'look after dear old mum' were the creation of the writers of *Dixon of Dock Green* many years later!

In rural areas, a typical copper might come across a wide range of criminality. Poaching was very common and had been a way of life for centuries. Tramps and drunks wandered the leafy lanes in search of a handout or a careless open window. Sheep stealing was a constant problem. So was bad behaviour at county fairs. Pickpockets, fraudsters, drunks and Irishmen were everywhere.

The country copper's urban counterpart had a bigger headache. Crime was more organized in towns and cities and in the ports, the arrival of men with little English and no knowledge of the country's laws added to the chaos. Before he became for ever associated with the hunt for Jack the Ripper, Frederick Abberline (see **Watching the Detectives**) was constantly coping with dog-stealing, pornography-selling and even cross-dressing! From time to time, scares broke out. The 1860s saw a rash of street crime in London and Birmingham based on the Indian cult of Thugee. Gangsters would work in pairs; one would loop a rope around a victim's throat while the other helped himself to any valuables. The Fenians (Irish nationalists) caused mayhem in the same decade and again in the 1880s by blowing up the police station at Clerkenwell and even damaging Scotland Yard. The on-going problems of drunkenness and prostitution kept any city copper busy night and day.

The police were always in the front line when it came to society 'demonstrating' for some change. It still goes on. As one Met officer described it to me a few years ago, there are always people who believe it is their right to 'save the unborn, gay whale'. The causes of the Victorians were more basic, to do with eating and human rights. But whether the cause was just or not, violence could erupt any minute. And the police were in the front line.

'Bloody Sunday' in November 1887 was a good example. A large crowd of socialists and radicals, heavily backed by working class toughs, congregated around Landseer's lions in Trafalgar Square to listen to various demagogues complaining because people weren't having it so good. 1,700 policemen were there, drawn up four-deep in some places, two-deep in others. The speeches began at 2.30pm and, as the mood grew uglier, 'spontaneous' attacks on the police broke out at four. Heavily outnumbered, the thin blue line held the swaying mob until the Commissioner of the Met, Sir Charles Warren (qv), ordered the Life Guards and the Foot Guards from their barracks to support them. Warren was criticised for his handling of the situation, but even the socialist William Morris, who was there, admitted that the actions of the police that day prevented even worse bloodshed and an all-out shoot out by the army.

By the end of the nineteenth century, there was almost an avuncular acceptance of the Old Bill. Lawson Wood's caricatures of the plump, red-faced, moustachioed copper, clipping kids around the ear for scrumping apples, belongs to twenty years later. His *Nine Pints of the Law* is particularly endearing. And it was true that society now regarded the police, by and large, as their friends. Only the villains saw them as the arch-enemy.

Technology transformed the police as it transformed crime. Typewriting machines* replaced hand-written reports during the 1880s. Telephone connection was set up,

---

* Purists, please note – a typewriter was originally someone, usually female, who operated such a machine (see **Going Postal**).

especially in the cities, in the following decade. The bicycle craze of the 1880s (see **Phew! It's a Scorcher!**) saw coppers on wheels for the first time, able to get to trouble spots as fast as the Mounted Division. The motor car revolutionized the country (see **Heigh Ho For the Open Road**). Not only were some forces driving Lanchesters and Morrises themselves (the famous Black Maria was no longer horse-drawn) but they were catching car thieves and, as early as 1905, setting up speed traps for the hooligans who hurtled around the country at a terrifying twenty-five miles an hour! There was no Highway Code until 1931 and speed limits varied (as they still do) according to the whim of the local authorities. Incidentally, the Automobile Association was prosecuted frequently in the early years of the new century for warning motorists about such speed traps.

There was a dogged heroism in the British police force of the Lestrade years. They were often unappreciated, more often unloved, but they were, in a world of change, necessary.

AIDING THE CIVIL POWER

Long before the creation of the regular British army (either in 1660 or 1685, take your pick) local defence units had been drawn up to protect their own area. The infantry were called Militia and the cavalry Yeomanry. The motto of several of these outfits was a reminder of their original purpose – *Pro Aris Et Focis,* For Hearths and Homes.

The Glamorgan Yeomanry was set up in 1797, when there was the very real likelihood of invasion by Revolutionary France. In fact, a French landing was made at Fishguard, Pembrokeshire, in the following year when a French man of war making for Ireland landed in the wrong place. Legend has it that a contingent of fishwives put the French to flight. The sight of the traditional red shawls and tall black hats of these Mumbles women reminded the French of British infantry and they ran for it, just as the Castlemartin (Pembrokeshire) Yeomanry turned up.

When they were not defending hearths and homes however, the Yeomanry were sometimes called upon to act as policemen, to 'aid the civil power' in the official jargon of the time. The men themselves hated this work because they were sometimes called upon to crack the heads of their friends and neighbours. That said, there was an element of class warfare in all this. Yeomanry soldiers (Other Ranks as well as officers) had to buy their uniforms and provide their own horses. Socially, in Glamorgan, the Yeomanry saw themselves as a cut above the miners who toiled at the coal face. The first time we see a clash between the two sides was at Tredegar in 1816, a year of bad harvests and incipient revolution.

On 19 October that year, a mob of 8,000 swarmed through the streets of Merthyr Tydfil, ignored the ironmaster's plea to return to work and turned deaf ears to the magistrates' Riot Act reading. The Swansea Yeomanry restored order with the flats of their swords. There were thirty arrests, but the only casualty was a dog cut in half by a Yeoman just to show how deadly the 1796 pattern Light Cavalry sabre could be!

The events depicted in the *Sign of Nine* in the context of the Glamorgan Yeomanry are fictional (See **Coca Cola with Maskelyne**) but they are based loosely on the Tonypandy riots of 1910. The years before the First World War, like those after the overthrow of Napoleon, were full of civil unrest as the relatively new trades unions flexed their muscles. There were serious riots among the miners of the Rhondda in November. The Chief Constable reported, 'Many casualties on both sides. Am expecting two companies of infantry and 200 cavalry today...Position grave.'

The cavalry were sent in on the orders of Winston Churchill (qv), the Home Secretary, a man whose reputation is still low in the Valleys, along with drafts of infantry and police. Common sense prevailed among the miners' leaders and the military and by 15 November, a 'friendly' football match was played. Everybody breathed a sigh of relief (not least the ref!).

THE MAN WHO CREATED THE CRIME NOVEL

Any of us who are practitioners of the Whodunit owes a huge debt of gratitude to William Wilkie Collins. The 'Master of Sensation' seems a little old hat now, but in his day he was the equal of Dickens and middle England couldn't get enough of his twisting plots and realistic characters.

His dad was a famous artist, a true-blue Tory and a pillar of the church. Young Wilkie was anything but. Born in Hampstead in January 1824, he never quite lost the 'baby' look. His enormous head was malformed, with one temple bulging and the other depressed. He had tiny hands and feet and was incredibly short-sighted. Undoubtedly a bright boy, he hated school and his dad was too mean to send him to Oxford. He dreamed of a life of sea-faring derring-do and so, of course, became a clerk in a company of tea-brokers – well, the stuff *did* come from overseas!

By the age of nineteen, Collins was writing rubbishy stories for the penny dreadfuls, a sort of graphic novels of their day. Publishers weren't interested. He studied law at Lincoln's Inn, but never practised and wrote his father's biography after Collins senior died in 1847. He made £100 and was at last noticed by the publishing world. The hundred quid, by the way, went on women, champagne and haute cuisine in Paris.

His novel *Antonia* left him comfortable and he lived with mummy in Blandford Square, enjoying the company of his brother's artist friends, John Millais and William Holman Hunt. He also met Dickens (one of the very few 'greats' that Lestrade never knew) and the great novelist encouraged the younger man to throw off the shackles of convention. He did this well and truly on a summer's night in 1854 when walking home from a party with Millais. There was a scream in a house they passed and a woman in white came hurtling out...the rest you know. She was Caroline Greaves who became Collins' mistress, despite her marrying Mr Clow the Plumber, who was certainly not a character from the card game Happy Families.

In the meantime, Collins had taken up with the hearty Martha Rudd who bore his three children; but he didn't live with her and Caroline Clow moved in with him in 1871. The man was a money machine – he got an advance of 5,000 guineas (half a million today, give or take) before he wrote a word in 1862 and cleared £10,000 the following year (well over a million in today's terms).

Behind the suave, successful womaniser, however, lay a tormented soul. Collins put the hypo into hypochondriac and spent most of his last twenty years in bed surrounded by medicine bottles. He became a morphine addict, hitting the laudanum big time – his biggest success, *The Moonstone*, was certainly written under the influence. The public loved him but the critics didn't and he became the forgotten man, terrified that he would read his own obituary in the Press. He died of a heart attack three years after *The Sign of Nine* and was buried in a common plot at Kensal Green cemetery.

'For there is good news yet to hear and fine things
to be seen,
   Before we go to Paradise by way of Kensal Green.'
G.K. Chesterton

BORLEY: THE MOST HAUNTED HOUSE IN ENGLAND

Obsessed with the trappings of death and the Spirit World, it was almost inevitable that the Victorians would create the haunted house. Britain is the most spook-ridden country in the world and although stories of apparitions and things going bump in the night stretch back into history, it was the nineteenth century that made such places tourist resorts.

The village of Borley lies on the Suffolk-Essex border and over the centuries went through a number of hands. It belonged to Benedictine monks in the 1360s and was owned by the Waldegrave family for three hundred years. In 1862, the Reverend H.D.E. Bull became rector of Borley and built a house for himself on the site of the old monastery.

In 1886, the year of the *Sign of Nine*, odd happenings began to occur. A spectral figure in a nun's habit was seen in the orchard and near the summer house. On more than one occasion, a coach and horses thundered silently through the grounds. Mrs Bull, the rector's wife, saw a huge bat-like creature in one of the house's myriad passageways. The Reverend Bull was one of a large number of Victorian clergymen who embraced spiritualism (see **Was Anybody There?**) and he held séances in the summerhouse. Via a spirit guide called Sunex Amures (only two letters away from the Latin for 'dirty old man'), the Bulls were able to learn, via the usual 'knock once for yes' routine, the explanation for the wandering nun. She was Marie Lairre, once a novice at the local convent who had fallen in love with a monk (said Sunex) and they had run away together in the coach and horses. No one ever explained where the big bat came in! Such carryings on were frowned upon in the fourteenth century, so Sunex was executed and Marie walled up alive in the convent.

Long after Lestrade's tangle with the place, the hauntings continued. In the summer of 1929 the new incumbent, the Rev G.E. Smith, contacted the *Daily Mirror* that was running a series on the supernatural. They sent Harry Price, the celebrated ghost-hunter, to investigate. Price was nearly as dodgy as the crooked or misguided souls he was investigating and he reported all sorts of poltergeist activity – bells ringing, doors slamming, pebbles cascading down the stairs. The focus of the activity was the Blue Room (hasn't everybody got one?) and Price held séances there, first with Smith, then with his successor, the Rev Lionel Foyster and his young (and possibly homicidal) wife, Marianne.

Throughout the Foyster tenancy, the spirit activities went off the scale. Not only did Price confirm the Marie Lairre story, he also witnessed the poor girl's attempts to save her soul. On the walls of the Blue Room, spirit writing occurred – 'Marie. Help. Light. Mass.' Clearly, Price explained in newspaper articles and the two books he wrote on the subject, this was the tragic nun asking for light in her pitch-black tomb and for a Mass to be said for her.

When Price rented the rectory in the late 1930s, he employed students from Cambridge University to spend the night in the house and the summer house, recording everything they saw, heard and felt. He even found human bones in a disused well under the kitchen floor. Borley Rectory mysteriously burned down on 27 February 1939, after which various strange lights were seen in the church across the road.

On a personal note, I once knew one of those Cambridge students employed by Price. He was Dr Allen Brown, lecturer in Medieval History at King's College, London and he was there after the fire, in the ruins of the house. On the first night, nothing happened and Brown and his colleagues wrote nothing in their notebooks. On the second night, all three of them distinctly heard heavy footsteps in the room above the ground floor where they were keeping watch. They decided to wait until dawn to investigate the room above. But, of course, the building was a ruin; there was no room above...

THE RIPPER

1888
'Oh, have you seen the Devil...?'

*I*n the year 1888, London was horrified by a series of brutal killings. All the victims were discovered in the same district, Whitechapel, and they were all prostitutes. But they weren't the only murders to perplex the brains of Scotland Yard. In Brighton, the body of one Edmund Gurney was also found.

Foremost among the Yard's top men was the young Inspector Sholto Lestrade and it was to his lot that the unsolved cases of a deceased colleague fell. Cases that included the murder of Martha Tabram, formerly a prostitute from Whitechapel, and that of the aforementioned Gurney.

Leaving no stone unturned, Lestrade investigates with his customary expertise and follows the trail to Nottinghamshire, to a minor public school, Rhadegund Hall. It is his intention to question the Reverend Algernon Spooner. What he finds is murder.

As the Whitechapel murders increase in number, so do those at Rhadegund Hall and so do the clues. What is the connection between them all? As if it weren't confusing enough, Lestrade is hampered by the parallel investigations of that great detective, Sherlock Holmes, aided by Dr Watson. Who is the murderer of Rhadegund Hall and are he and the man they call 'Jack the Ripper' one and the same?

THE WHITECHAPEL MURDERS

Between August and November 1888, a number of women, all prostitutes, were murdered by an unknown assailant christened by the Press as Jack the Ripper.

The area was notorious as a centre of vice and violence but Jack's crimes stood apart from this in terms of the ferocity and nature of the murders themselves. Two Divisions of the Met, H and J, hunted Jack in a search co-ordinated by Scotland Yard and when one victim died in the City of London, the City police entered the fray too.

The jury is still out on exactly how many women the Whitechapel murderer actually killed. Sir Melville Macnaghten (qv), who became Assistant Commissioner of the Met in June 1889, claimed there were five and that was the number I used in *Lestrade and the Ripper*. When I wrote the book to coincide with the centenary of the murders, everything included was the cutting edge of research. Nearly thirty years later, we now know a great deal more about the sort of man Jack was, thanks to research into the forensic psychology of serial killers, mostly in the United States. We also know a great deal more about his victims. To avoid confusion, I will cover here only Macnaghten's 'canonical five'.

In the early hours of Friday 31 August, 43-year-old Mary Ann (Polly) Nichols was found dead in Buck's Row (now Durward Street) Whitechapel by a carman on his way to work. The police were summoned and took the body to the Whitechapel Workhouse mortuary where the police surgeon, Dr Llewellyn, carried out a post mortem. Her throat had been cut and there were various mutilations to the abdomen. Polly had probably been strangled first and the cuts indicated a right-handed person with some rough medical knowledge. The inquest resulted in the usual 'murder by some person or persons unknown'.

Eight days later (Saturday 8 September) as John Davis was on his way to work in Spitalfields Market, he noticed a body lying next to steps that led into the yard at the back of 29, Hanbury Street. It was that of 47-year-old Annie Chapman, known as 'Dark Annie', at a spot frequently used by prostitutes and their clients. Dr Bagster Phillips, carrying out his post mortem in the Whitechapel Workhouse mortuary, concluded that Annie too had been strangled. Her throat had been cut so deeply that he believed there had been an attempt to decapitate her. The mutilations to her abdomen were more severe than in the Nichols case and the intestines were laid out alongside the body. The uterus, bladder and part of the vagina had been removed. Again, there were signs of medical knowledge. Despite various clues at the murder scene (some of which had nothing to do with Annie's death) the inquest could only return the usual verdict.

It was not until Sunday 30 September that the Whitechapel killer struck again, but when he did, the details of the 'double event' struck terror into the hearts of East Enders and sent both the local and national Press into overdrive. Louis Diemschutz was a pedlar returning from a hard day on the road. His pony shied at the entrance to Dutfield's Yard in Berner Street and, dismounting from the trap, Diemschutz found the body of 43-year-old Elizabeth

Stride, known as Long Liz. She had been strangled and her throat cut, but there were no mutilations. Diemschutz dashed up nearby steps to the Whitechapel Working Men's Educational Club to get help. It was possible that while he was gone, Liz's killer was hiding behind the gate and could make good his escape. If he did, he must have moved west because forty-five minutes later, he struck again.

The second victim of the double event was Catherine (Kate) Eddowes, 46, found butchered in Mitre Square, in the jurisdiction of the City of London. The police provided a complete inventory of Kate's possessions and the police surgeon, Dr Brown, drew a detailed sketch both at the crime scene and later as part of his very thorough post mortem. Kate had been found by a patrolling copper, PC Edward Watkins, in the darkest corner of the square. Her throat had been cut and later investigation proved that her uterus and one kidney had been removed. There were also lacerations to the face. The fact that this murder had taken place between two police patrols, only twenty minutes apart and that the mutilations had been carried out in total darkness, gave Jack an almost superhuman notoriety and panic set in.

For the first time, there was a real clue; a portion of Kate's apron had been cut off and was found at a standpipe in nearby Goulston Street. Clearly, the murderer had wiped his hands with it and the site suggested that he was on his way home, to the East End.

Over the years, doubts have crept in about the double event. The fact that Liz Stride had not been mutilated is perhaps evidence of *two* killers at work that night. Most people (Lestrade included!) do not believe in coincidences like this.

The last of the canonical five, Mary Jane Kelly, who had a number of aliases, died in the early hours of Friday 9

November, Lord Mayor's Day. Her murder is different from the others because she was only twenty-five and was killed indoors, in her dingy single room in 13, Miller's Court, off Dorset Street. Rent collector Thomas Bowyer called on Mary mid-morning because she owed several weeks' rent. He could see her appallingly-mutilated body through the broken window of Number 13 and called the police. Dr Thomas Bond reported that Mary's throat had been cut, her breasts removed and her face was slashed so as to make it unrecognizable. Her intestines were draped around the furniture and even under her body. Her heart was missing.

A fire in the grate (possibly lit to give the killer maximum light to work by) had charred portions of a woman's clothes. It was not known whether these were Mary's or not.

Because of the ferocity of the Miller's Court murder, the assumption was made at the time that this marked the 'pinnacle' of Jack's frenzy. The fact that no murders of this ferocity happened later (not *quite* true) led others to believe that the Whitechapel murderer took his own life soon afterwards or was incarcerated for another crime altogether.

The media was always working at fever pitch as the body count escalated. Hoax letters were sent to the police and the Press and over 200 suspects were arrested and eliminated. Eventually, the dust settled and the world moved on, ready to embrace a whole industry devoted to Jack the Ripper (see **The House That Jack Built**).

THE ABYSS

By the time of the Ripper murders, Whitechapel and Spitalfields were known as the Ghetto or the Abyss. A number of people from Jack London to Israel Zangwill, were fascinated by the place and wrote about it extensively. Given its mix of racial alienation, poverty and high crime rate, it is difficult to think of a more likely setting for Jack's stalking grounds.

The Irish moved out as the Jews moved in. There were still many Irishmen around in 1888. John McCarthy owned 26, Dorset Street, the home of Mary Kelly; Timothy Donovan ran Crossingham's doss house down the road. But it was the Jewishness of the area that struck visitors. Pogroms in Russia and Poland in the early to mid-1880s drove thousands of Ashkenazi Jews westward. Some paused briefly in London before moving on to America, but others stayed. Many of them set up in the rag trade, selling old clothes in Petticoat Lane (Middlesex Street), squeezing out the older generations of weavers who had settled there. Most of those people worked hard, but a living was difficult to come by. Sometimes witnesses to Jack's – and other people's – crimes, they were often loath to talk to the police. Their English was poor and they had an understandable fear of uniformed men in authority. There was resentment from the original locals who referred to 'the

Jews of Whitechapel, cutting our throats all along' five years before Jack struck.

The area was close to the London Docks, then the largest in the world and drunkenness and violence went hand in hand with poverty. Dock work was well paid but hard to get; one man who had not found a job in eighteen months killed his wife and four children with a penknife, then waited quietly for the police to arrest him. All of Jack's victims, whether we accept Macnaghten's 'canonical' five or opt for a more likely larger figure, were actual or borderline alcoholics. There were twenty-six public houses in the tiny area centring on Flower and Dean Street and yet more off-licences that broke the law by selling at all hours of the day and night. Both Mary Kelly and Annie Chapman drank at the Britannia at the corner of Commercial and Dorset Streets. George Lusk of the Whitechapel Vigilance Committee held regular meetings at the Crown in the Mile End Road. Polly Nichols went to her death from the Frying Pan in Brick Lane. Liz Stride was a regular at the Queen's Head in Commercial Street and the Ten Bells, up the road from the rough sleeping ground of 'Itchy Park', was for several years at the end of the twentieth century, renamed the Jack the Ripper.

The prostitutes and down-and-outs who wandered the grease-scummed streets and pestered passers-by, usually had no fixed abode. Some 'carried the banner', sleeping rough in doorways. Those who could afford it raised the 4d required for a single bed in a flea-infested dormitory in one of the dozens of doss or common lodging houses in the area. Mary Kelly dossed at Cooley's in Thrawl Street before finding her accommodation at McCarthy's Rents in Miller's Court. Kate Eddowes had breakfast at Cooney's (confusing or what?) at 55, Flower and Dean on her last morning. Annie

Chapman often stayed at Crossingham's in Dorset Street. Polly Nichols was briefly at the White House, 56, Flower and Dean.

The whole area was a rabbit warren of alleyways and courts where prostitutes plied their trade. There were gangs in the area like the High Rips, who may or may not have attacked Emma Smith on the night of 3 April 1888; and the Nichol gang who operated out of the streets to the north. It was no accident that the Kray twins, many years later, came from Whitechapel. Vallance Road, where they lived in the 'fortress' with their mum, was called Baker's Row in Jack's day and led to both the Jews' Burial Ground and the Whitechapel Workhouse.

THE HOUSE THAT JACK BUILT

The first full book on the Whitechapel murders was the Swedish *Hvem Ar Jack Uppskararen?* (Who Was Jack the Ripper?) in 1889. Its existence at once proved the fascination with unsolved crime and the international dimension of the research. The French call him Jacques L'Eventreur; the Spanish El Destripador; the Welsh moniker is Jakrippa.

Since 1889, work on Jack has grown to a vast industry. There have been articles, books (fact and fiction), films (movies and documentaries), graphic novels and even a musical. All over the world, thousands of people call themselves Ripperologists, argue minutiae in chatrooms, attend conferences and have their pet theories.

Because the Whitechapel murderer was never caught, the assumption has been made by some that he was so powerful, so important, so well known, that the police were barred from investigating him. In the mad world of conspiracy theories, Jack the Ripper is king. The real reason that the killer was never caught is that he was a new breed – the blitz serial murderer – of a type the police had never encountered before (See **The Habitual Homicide**). He got away with his crimes because he was low profile, of the same (anonymous) class as his victims and he knew the area like the back of his hand. He was also – and this applies to all criminals who evade capture – extraordinarily lucky.

But the lunatic fringe of Ripperologists will have none of this. The medical knowledge hinted at by some police surgeons at the time means that he has to be a mad doctor, with or without a syphilitic son, who had sworn vengeance on the diseased women of the East End. Because Whitechapel was 95 per cent Jewish immigrants, Jack must be an Eastern European; better, he has to be a Russian homicidal maniac in the pay of the Tsar's government. Nonsense, say others. The medical thing points to a bungling midwife (abortions then being backstreet and illegal) bent on covering up her ineptitude. In our celebrity-obsessed age, Jack must have been a Famous Person. So he was the artist Walter Sickert, the philanthropist (and doctor, don't forget!) Thomas Barnardo. He was the Prince of Wales (qv). He was Lewis Carroll, creator of the Alice fantasies. He was Lord Randolph Churchill, father of the future Prime Minister. He was William Gladstone (qv)(somebody might have a point there!). He was Leopold II, king of the Belgians – well, he *was* rather beastly to the natives of the Congo!

Alternatively, he could have been a policeman – how easy to suppress vital evidence. Charles Warren's (qv) name is writ large here, as the bungling Commissioner who resigned the day before Mary Kelly was killed. What about other established murderers? The poisoner Neill Cream, perhaps? Or the family killer, Frederick Deeming? You might care to throw in a murder victim, like James Maybrick, the unpleasant Liverpool cotton merchant poisoned by his wife. Then there are a whole host of locals (and I believe we are getting warmer here) behaving oddly at the time – Michael Ostrog, John Pizer, Aaron Kosminski. There are many more, but there is no hard evidence against any of them.

For sheer nonsense, however, you can't do better than journalist Stephen Knight's 1976 *The Final Solution*. It was neither final nor a solution but it is *the* book on Jack that caught the public's imagination. It had conspiracy (those devious bêtes noires, the Freemasons); the royals (Prince Albert Victor unwisely dipping his wick among the working classes); a mad doctor (the Queen's Physician in ordinary, Sir William Gull); and the aforementioned Walter Sickert as lookout. If you want a serious discussion on the Whitechapel murders, read anything by Paul Begg, Philip Sugden, Stewart Evans or (and I blush with modesty) M.J. Trow. If you want a laugh, read Stephen Knight.

THE LADIES OF THE NIGHT

The Victorian middle classes were masters of the euphemism. Polite society surrounded itself with coy language that made today's politically correct lobby sound like navvies. Breasts (shudder!) were 'baby's public house'; legs (gasp!) were 'nether regions'. Because France was supposedly the centre of all things vice-related, French terms were substituted for the real thing. A woman who ran a brothel was a 'Madame'; the brothel itself a 'Bordello' (actually a Spanish word that had crept over the Pyrenees). Upper class prostitutes were 'les grandes horizontales'; the social group below them, the 'demi-monde'. Sex in general was a taboo subject. Put succinctly, the Victorians did it but they didn't talk about it.

'Nice' girls went into marriage not only as virgins but having no idea about what went on in the bedroom. While Victoria (qv) herself was so head-over-heels (one of the rarer Victorian positions) in love with Albert, her mother had famously advised her to 'lie back and think of England'. Thousands of girls of lesser births had no such aspirational hopes; neither did all of them find sexual bliss. Divorce was unthinkable, so unhappy marriages abounded.

Men were different. The feminist lobby fully believed they were all beasts and the war of the sexes produced ludicrous stereotypes. *He* was only after one thing. *She* was no better than she should be. Other than abstinence (which did *not* make the heart grow fonder), there was no effective birth control and pregnancy and childbirth carried far more dangers than today. A middle class man was expected to marry someone suitable, an 'adornment to her sex', preferably a wealthy woman who would make a good mother. Fun in the bedroom could be provided elsewhere – and this is where prostitution came in.

There is no doubt that the Victorians were worried about prostitution, as they were about drunkenness (see **The Demon Drink**). Both were endemic in society at all levels. The difference was that drunkenness could be discussed publicly; sex could not. Journalists like William Stead (qv); evangelists like William Booth (qv); reformers like Annie Besant risked, and in two cases underwent, prison sentences merely for printing material that today would not turn a hair.

Prostitution was a class thing. Collectively called 'scarlet sisters', 'unfortunates' and 'ladies of the night', each social group was proud of its status and offered a service as real as hoteliers or restaurant owners. When William Booth carried out his research among them for *In Darkest England and the Way Out* (1891) he found very few who regretted the career they had chosen and equally few who claimed they were driven onto the streets by poverty. All five of Jack the Ripper's victims began adult life as 'respectable'; a series of setbacks, separations from the men in their lives and drunkenness put them in harm's way, not poverty itself.

At the top were the kept women, fashionable ladies from genteel families. The best known was Catherine Walters ('Skittles') the mistress of the Prince of Wales (qv), who was a notorious bed-hopper. They spoke French, played the piano and sang, were dab hands at needlepoint and could be admired with their 'fancy Dans' riding in Rotten Row every morning in their exquisitely tailored habits. They were passed from earl to viscount until their looks deteriorated and were then largely discarded. The next time you are in London's West End, go to Oxford Street and turn off into Duke St or James St. These were their houses, where they had servants and usually a stable for their carriage and pair.

Below them came the denizens of the brothels. The most famous Madame in the 1860s was Kate Hamilton, whose establishment in the Haymarket catered for all tastes. A man-about-town could enjoy a meal here, washed down with his favourite bubbly before selecting a girl for the night – two, of course, cost extra.

At the bottom of the heap came the soldiers' women and the park girls. Army towns attracted camp followers – still a sizeable problem in the Second World War – and the army itself was responsible for their existence. Actual marriage was frowned on by the authorities, so that army 'wives' were actually nothing of the sort. If the regiment was posted overseas (for example, to the Crimea or India) most women were turfed out into the street and the army took no responsibility for them (see **Soldiers of the Queen**).

This flotsam and jetsam formed the target group of the Whitechapel murderer, but vast numbers of them were the victims of drunken brutality. Frederick Charrington, heir to a vast brewery fortune, turned his back on the family money because of the damage that drunkenness could do. He once witnessed a girl being kicked to death in the street under the very hoarding that carried his father's name. Henry Mayhew discussed these women obliquely in his pioneering social research in 1850. William Booth both wrote about them directly forty years later. Women like this rarely had a fixed abode – of Jack's victims, only Mary Kelly had a room and she was way behind on the rent for it. The others drifted from doss house to doss house, earning the fourpence required for a bed with sex in the street from passing punters.

One of the worst aspects of the sex trade from today's perspective was child prostitution. In 1889, the age of consent was fixed at thirteen; before that, it didn't exist. Boys and girls from the country were lured into the sex trade as easily and as often as Oliver Twist in Dickens' 1838 novel was lured into picking pockets. Superintendent Dunlap of C Division was very concerned that it was rife on his patch, but everywhere else was just as bad. Children were a commodity for poor families and it was a difficult call to make whether a child was better off on the streets or suffocating up a chimney or in a sweat-shop. Various 'guides' were available in the 1870s which advertised girls as young as nine, with a list of their 'accomplishments'.

From time to time the police of the cities and larger towns – prostitution was largely an urban problem – rounded up prostitutes and let them sleep off their drunkenness in a cell overnight. Actual prosecutions were rare – and prosecutions of punters were rarer still.

THE HABITUAL HOMICIDE

One reason that Jack got away with his crimes was that he represented a new kind of murderer – the serial killer. The phrase did not exist in Victorian England; the term for someone who killed more than once was habitual homicide.

Everyone expected such a man to be a dribbling, wild-eyed maniac, whose irrational behaviour would make him easily found. Sexually-motivated crimes were not fully understood. Henry Havelock Ellis wrote *The Criminal* in 1907, but the most comprehensive work was Richard Krafft-Ebing's *Psychopathia Sexualis* (1892). A handful of policemen, like Chief Inspector John Littlechild, had read Krafft-Ebing but probably very few rank and file coppers had and the patrolling constables had no idea what to look for.

In the medico-legal world, the most authoritative text was *L'Uomo Delinquente* (Criminal Man) by Cesare Lombroso. He and other 'experts' believed that criminals could be identified by their physical characteristics. Sex offenders usually had full beards and rectilinear noses. Lunatics were often bald. Rapists were fair-haired and blue-eyed. The habitual homicide (an extremely rare breed, it seems, in 1888) had a fixed, glassy stare. His nose was often beaked, his jaws strong. He had long ears, high cheekbones and dark, curly hair. His lips were thin and his canine teeth much developed. If all this sounds rather like a werewolf or a vampire, that was because such fantasies from central Europe were in vogue. None of it bore any relation to actual serial killers at all.

Today we have the opportunity of studying such people in detail. 74 per cent of them are American and they may languish for years on Death Row awaiting execution or are in mental institutions. Forensic psychological studies called profiling have thrown up the typical behaviour patterns of a blitz-style sex killer (of which Jack was perhaps the first). Such studies, however, stress that there is no such thing as 'typical' – aberrations abound.

Experts today identify six phases in the MO of a serial killer:

1. The aura phase – the wannabe killer fantasizes on a crime and withdraws into his own private world.
2. The trolling phase – the killer seeks to put his plans into practice, selecting his victim according to his own criteria (physical appearance, behaviour or even location).
3. The wooing phase – the killer makes contact with his victim – in the case of Jack, no doubt, by posing as a client.
4. The capture phase – the killer strikes – in the Whitechapel cases, perhaps from behind, partial strangulation followed by throat-slitting and mutilations.
5. The totem phase – many serial killers take away a memento – Kate Eddowes' kidney; Mary Kelly's heart – to keep and relive the moment of the murder.

6. The depression phase – all passion spent, the killer becomes despondent but after an indeterminate time, the whole cycle begins again.

None of this was understood by anybody during the Autumn of Terror.

SIR CHARLES WARREN

Charles Warren, Commissioner of the Met at the time of the Ripper murders, has had a bad press. That's because he deserves it. He was one of a long line of senior men recruited from the army because it was (wrongly) believed that only military men could run a police force.

Educated at Cheltenham (*not* the Ladies' College, despite the rumours) he went down the Engineers path via Sandhurst and Woolwich (the 'Shop') before obtaining his commission in 1857. A keen amateur archaeologist (see **the Testimony of the Spade**) – they were all amateur then – Warren wrote three books on the subject while serving in Palestine. He fought in the Kaffir War 1877-8 and was back home by 1880 running the Army Engineering School at Chatham. Along with everybody else, he got to Khartoum too late to save General Gordon and was appointed Commissioner in 1886.

A number of pro-Warren books written recently try to excuse him by saying that he was 'unlucky' in the policemen and politicians with whom he had to work, but is it likely they were all out of step and he wasn't? The media and the public loathed him. He was in sympathy with Irish dissidents at a time when such men were blowing up parts of London – even Scotland Yard – with dynamite. It is difficult to avoid the charge that Warren was a man ahead of his time; 'sensitive' policing was not going to work in Victorian England.

To be fair, nothing good was going to come out of 'Bloody Sunday' whatever Warren did. On 13 November 1887, a huge crowd of the unemployed gathered in Trafalgar Square. Polite society, horrified by such a sea of the great unwashed, demanded they be cleared out. They were, by the police and the army. The other half of polite society, Gladstone's pinko-liberals, were outraged at the heavy handedness of the Met. For Warren, it was lose-lose.

Involved in political in-fighting with the Home Office and his own senior officers, he made rash pronouncements to the Press – for example, an article on policing London in *Murray's Magazine* – had his knuckles rapped and resigned.

The fact that this became known on the morning that Mary Kelly's body was found inevitably linked these events in the minds of the media and public. Warren had been fired, people believed, over his failure to catch Jack.

Whatever Warren's shortcomings as a policeman, they pale into insignificance with his later performance as a soldier. Returning to the army, he made a complete hash of things against the Boers at Spion Kop in 1900. All in all, not a happy bunny.

CHARLES BRADLAUGH
(PR. BRADLEE)

B radlaugh was a maverick, born out of time and as stubborn as a mule. He hailed from Hoxton, London and took a number of lowly clerical jobs after leaving school at eleven. He was dismissed from a teaching job for his atheism at a time when such a stand was unacceptable – he got off lightly; in Shakespeare's day, they burned people for that! He joined the army briefly before returning to London in 1853 as a free thinker. Freedom of thought was something the Victorians disliked – conformity and tradition tried to hold the line in a rapidly changing world.

Bradlaugh became President of the Secular Society in 1858 and edited with Annie Besant, champion of women's rights, the secular *National Reformer*. For that, both of them were tried for blasphemy and sedition. Bradlaugh got off, but ten years later, the pair's sensible work on birth control – the *Fruits of Philosophy or the Private Companion of Young Married People* – landed them in court again. And again, in a storm of Press agitation, Bradlaugh escaped gaol.

In a way, the 'man who denied God' was like the Marlon Brando character in the film *The Wild One*. When asked what he was protesting about, he said, 'What have you got?' Bradlaugh backed the Trades Unions and Women's

Suffrage (see **Votes For Women**). He supported the Irish over Home Rule. He backed the French in the Franco-Prussian War of 1870. He drew a line however in that he opposed Socialism – there were, after all, standards!

In 1880, Bradlaugh outraged almost everybody by winning an election for Northamptonshire and refusing to swear the necessary oath of allegiance to take his place in the Commons. 'To me,' he said, 'the word "God" standing alone is a word without meaning.' The attack on him was spearheaded by another, but very different, maverick, Lord Randolph Churchill and he was imprisoned briefly in the little cell (I bet you didn't know there was one) under Big Ben. Three times Bradlaugh won the by-election and each time was denied his seat in the Commons. By 1886, common sense prevailed and he was allowed to affirm rather than swear the oath, which effectively carried parliament kicking and screaming into the twentieth century.

The Public Schools

Rhadegund Hall does not exist but it represents the real 'top' schools to which the sons of gentlemen were sent to acquire a good education.

Though by no means the oldest (and tradition, in such schools, was everything) Winchester (1382) is regarded as the *fons et origo* (fount and original). It was eclipsed however by Eton and Harrow and later, once the sport caught on, Rugby. Families sent their sons to these expensive, fee-paying establishments generation after generation and the notion that they were once for *any* boy and *free* disappeared into the snobbery of elitism.

Typically, a boy from the upper classes would be taught at home by a nanny or governess. At the age of seven, he would be sent away to Prep (preparatory) school. He could already read and write by then and he was taught the basics of a classical education which was thought to be essential for the gentleman of a civilized society. At fourteen, he attended the public school of choice and got stuck in to Latin, Greek and mathematics. Those were taught by rote and scarcely encouraged a boy to think at all. The staff, known universally as Masters, wore academic gowns and mortar boards as scholars had for centuries, and most of them applied the cane with vigour.

Outside the classroom, the boy was left largely to his own devices, policed by the larger and older pupils in the prefectorial system or boy government. There was a great deal of brutality and bullying here, along the lines of *Lord of the Flies* until Dr Thomas Arnold, Head of Rugby School, imposed his authority and insisted the prefects report to him daily. It doesn't say much for educational attainment, however, that Arnold was less concerned with learning than turning out 'Christian gentlemen'.

Even so, the system worked. Even though less than one per cent of the nation's boys attended public school, they formed nearly 80 per cent of politicians, government employees, officers of the armed forces and leading churchmen. The fagging system, by which younger boys acted as unpaid servants to older ones, instilled a sense of obedience and the ability to take orders. In their turn, as the fags became prefects, they learned to give orders and ultimately, to run an empire. Eton, for example, has produced nineteen prime ministers and one reason, apart from his Jewishness, that Benjamin Disraeli (qv) was always considered by some to be an outsider, is that he did not attend public school.

The Adventures of Inspector Lestrade

1891
'Such as these shall never look
At this pretty picture book.'

*I*t is 1891 and London is still reeling from the horror of the unsolved Ripper murders when Inspector Lestrade (that 'ferret-like' anti-hero so often out-detected by the legendary Sherlock Holmes) is sent to the Isle of Wight to investigate a strange corpse found walled up in Shanklin Chine.

But this is only the start of the nightmare. It is merely the beginning of a series of killings so brutal, so bizarre and, apparently, so random, that only a warped genius – and a master of disguise – could be responsible. Even when Lestrade pieces together the extraordinary pattern behind the crimes from the anonymous poems sent after each murder, he is no closer to knowing the identity of the sinister, self-styled 'Agrippa', the 'great, long, red-legg'd scissor-man'.

It becomes a very personal battle and Lestrade's desperate race to avert the next death in the sequence takes him all over the country, from London to the Pennines and back, resulting in a portfolio of suspects which covers the entire range of late-Victorian society.

Alfred, Lord Tennyson

Tennyson was a vicar's son from Lincolnshire, born in the same year as Gladstone (qv). After attendance at various grammar schools, the boy went up to Trinity College, Cambridge where he joined the Apostles, an intellectual student group only ever twelve in number. He published his first poems in 1830, followed by *The Lady of Shalott* three years later. Perhaps it was the awful ' "Tirra-lirra by the river", sang Sir Lancelot' that put readers off; the book was heavily criticised and Tennyson wrote nothing for ten years.

He was pretty broke when he moved to London in 1842 and produced a new poetry book, including the brilliant *Break, Break, Break*, immortalising the untimely death of his friend Arthur Hallam. This and subsequent works gave him financial security and he bought Farringford, a country house in the Isle of Wight, in 1856. Pursued by tourists (not to mention his nosey neighbour, the photographer Julia Margaret Cameron) he only wintered there after 1869 when there were fewer tourists.

In 1850, the Queen (God Bless Her) appointed him Poet Laureate – the immortal *Charge of the Light Brigade* was one of his 'jobs' and a peerage followed. Victoria found his poems soothing and met him twice, enchanted by his tall, dark appearance, complete with long hair, wideawake hat and long cloak.

Other poets, of his day and later, have been very bitchy about him. Robert Browning thought he was 'mentally infirm'. T.S. Eliot found him sad; W.H. Auden believed him 'stupid'.*

---

* What did he know?

LAURENCE ALMA-TADEMA

One of the most successful painters of the Victorian period, Lourens was born in Dronrijp in the Netherlands in 1836 and studied at Antwerp's Royal Academy. He settled in London in 1870, because at the height of the Franco-Prussian War, Belgium was not the place to be.*

Throughout the '60s and '70s, Alma-Tadema produced huge canvases, usually with historic themes. The Merovingians (French kings of the Dark Ages) caught his artist's eye; so did the ancient Egyptians. By 1879, he was a fully exhibited member of the British Royal Academy and spent the '80s wandering around archaeological sites like Rome and Pompeii sketching for various Roman projects. *The Roses of Heliogabalus* is one (1888), *The Coliseum* (1896) and *The Baths of Caracalla* (1899) were two more.

As a person, he was mischievous, with a short temper and a penchant for practical jokes. In some ways, he remained a child all his life. On the other hand, he was a consummate professional, sometimes taking up to four years to finish a canvas. He is buried in the crypt of St Paul's, having spent his declining years condemning

---

* It never is.

the nonsense of Post-Impressionism, Cubism, Fauvism and Futurism.

Incidentally, to any readers who are wannabe artists – 'stick to your trade, young gentlemen'; in 2011, Alma-Tadema's *The Meeting of Anthony and Cleopatra* sold at Sotheby's, New York, for $29.2 million.

KING EDWARD VII

He was 'Bertie', he was 'Rumty-Tum', he was 'the Uncle of Europe' and the 'Peacemaker'. As Prince of Wales and later King Edward VII, he was all things to all men (not to mention women). He held nine foreign military commissions and twenty foreign titles, including the Order of the White Elephant of Siam and the Order of the Golden Fleece which would have made his predecessor Elizabeth turn in her grave.*

Bertie was the eldest son of Victoria (qv) and Albert, born in Buckingham Palace in November 1841. He had umpteen titles as a toddler and was a Knight of the Garter at seventeen. Limited academically, Bertie suffered under a succession of tutors while his far more intellectual father tried to make a future king out of him. He went through the usual honorary university courses provided for royalty – Edinburgh, Oxford, Cambridge and went on his first royal tour, to Canada, in 1860. He bowled everybody over with his charm and affability, but for the rest of their lives, his parents ignored this admirable character trait and tried to make him into something he was not.

Losing his cherry to the 'actress' Nellie Clifden in Dublin (he was set up by his fellow officers at the army camp

---

* Not the same family, of course. The Tudors were Welsh; the Saxe-Coburgs German.

nearby) he became an international playboy even when married to the sweet, if deaf, Alexandra of Denmark. News of Bertie's womanising reached his father, already ill with (according to contemporary reports) typhoid. There was a row and Victoria ever after blamed the totally innocent Bertie for Albert's death.

With little to do in the way of official engagements – he opened the odd railway station, tunnel and sewerage facility – he became something of a fashion guru with his notions of how to press trousers, and leaving one's bottom waistcoat button undone. This last had little to do with fashion and a great deal to do with his increasing girth; Bertie loved good food, good wine, good cigars and bad women.

He followed the Turf, owning a number of racehorses, competed with his nephew the Kaiser (qv) in yachting fests off Cowes and produced two sons who, in different ways, were disappointments. The elder, 'old collar and cuffs', Albert Victor, died of 'flu in 1892** and the younger became the boring old fart, George V.

Sensitivity – and the fact that the author is still hoping for a gong from Her Majesty – forbids a list of Bertie's mistresses, but it was quite long. They ranged from titled ladies to Parisian tarts and were seen by Bertie as the perks of office.

He had 'appendicitis' (but see *Lestrade and the Hallowed House* for the real story) on the eve of his coronation, but recovered to become a breath of fresh air after Victoria and one of the most popular monarchs in history. His death in 1910 removed the one person who might *just* have been able to prevent the First World War.

** No, he was not involved in the Whitechapel murders in any shape or form. Neither was Walter Sickert, but that's another story altogether.

'General' William Booth

With his kind, twinkly eyes and long white beard, the founder of the Salvation Army looks as though he has just stepped out of the Old Testament.

Originally from a solid working-class family in Nottinghamshire, Booth became apprenticed to a pawnbroker (the sign of the three balls was well known to any working-class family at the time) and became a Methodist. A natural orator, he was preaching to Nottingham's down-and-outs in the 1840s and moved to London in search of work. He came into his own on the Mile End Waste, preaching to the poor outside the Blind Beggar Pub, later a murder scene in the Kray era.

Booth's message was simple – Jesus saves and he loves everybody. With his family in tow, Booth set up the Salvation Army in the summer of 1878. It had uniforms (black with a cherry trim), a simple message, leaflets (*The War Cry*), tambourines and singing. His book, *In Darkest England and the Way Out* (1891) was one of the few to address the then unmentionable problem of prostitution. It was still being reprinted in 2006.

People made fun of the movement, calling it the Skeleton Army, but the girls who went out from Angel Alley in Whitechapel to provide soup and salvation were a much needed palliative to the chronic poverty of the time.

In 1904, partially blind, the General took part in the first religious motorcade in Britain, preaching from his open-top car. He was 'promoted to Glory' as the Army had it in August 1912, a genuinely good man in an all-too-often bad time.*

*As a student in Cambridge, I lodged with an old gent who had had his hair ruffled by the General, back in the day. Ah, the continuity of History!

OSCAR WILDE

'The Great Queen was dead. All the years of tribulation – and the trials – over at last. The century had barely begun before the great heart had given up the ghost. And peace came. So much for Oscar Wilde.'
Lestrade and the Hallowed House

Anybody with the middle names Fingal O'Flahertie had a pretty tough furrow to plough. Even so, you don't have to make the meal of it that dear old Oscar did. He was bizarre, even by the standards of Victorian eccentrics and, as things turned out, was his own worst enemy.

He was a few months younger than Lestrade, born to intellectual parents in Dublin. Speaking fluent French and German, young Oscar went up to Trinity College, Dublin and Magdalen, Oxford to read Greats (Oxford's snobby term for Classical literature). He became involved in the Aesthetic movement – 'Art for Art's Sake' – which embraced the beautiful in poetry, painting and architecture and lectured on those themes in Canada and the United States. Famously claiming on one of these tours that, at Customs, he had 'nothing to declare but his genius', he dressed in anachronistic knee breeches and velvet jacket with a floppy, Neronian hairstyle that would not have looked amiss in Hugh Grant's Notting Hill a few years ago.

Wilde wrote essays, poems, plays and stories and became the darling of the London literati. While *The Picture of Dorian Grey* was suitably spooky, his greatest successes were the society comedies *The Importance of Being Earnest* and *Lady Windermere's Fan*.

Though happily married to Constance and with two children to his credit, Oscar's sexual interests lay elsewhere and it was his misfortune that the 'naughty nineties' weren't as naughty as all that. One of Wilde's friends was Lord Alfred Douglas ('Bosie') whose father was the repellent Marquess of Queensbury (he of the boxing rules). When Queensbury found out about his dalliance with his son, he sent Wilde a bouquet of rotting veg to the West End theatre where *Earnest* was playing with a card reading 'For Oscar Wilde, posing somdomite' (sic). Instead of leaving matters there, with ample proof of what an illiterate oaf Queensbury was, Wilde sued for criminal libel.

'The love that dare not speak its name' was illegal, thanks to Henry Labouchere's Criminal Law Amendment Act of 1884 and Wilde found himself in court on charges of gross indecency. The jury was hung but at the third trial, he was found guilty and sentenced to two years hard labour in Reading gaol. The ballad he wrote there is perhaps the best thing he ever produced.

Wilde never saw Bosie again and died, broken and half-forgotten in Paris in 1900. He is buried in a hideous tomb in the cemetery of Pere Lachaise, sharing his last resting place with a diverse bunch from Chopin to Jim Morrison – how appalling!

Religion

'Religion,' Karl Marx said, or near enough, 'is the opium of the people.' In various parts of Victorian London, opium was the opium of the people and eventually, in Russia, Marxism became the opium of the people. So, basically, it's a funny old world, isn't it?

Church of England

The Church of England dominated nineteenth century religion in all sorts of ways. Bishops sat in the House of Lords and the Church was a landowner on a massive scale, owning not merely the buildings and churchyards but 'glebe' land all over the country. Rents from this were astronomic, long before they charged admission to various cathedrals and minsters. Careers in the Church were open to men only and it was usually the stupidest member of a genteel family who would become a man of the cloth. He would emerge from Oxford or Cambridge with a degree in Divinity and find a living, usually somewhere nice.

In country areas, the squire and the parson still ran the show and the vicarage was often a large, rambling house, with stables and servants, at a peppercorn rent. Conscientious vicars did the rounds, tending the sick and the old, looking out for the material as well as spiritual needs of their flock. Most however just worked on Sundays and officiated at the hatch, match and dispatch of their parishioners as the need arose.

There was some muscular Christianity. Vicars like Samuel Barnett of Whitechapel deliberately chose tough inner-city parishes, with tiny congregations and little thanks for their trouble. It was because there were so few of these that General William Booth (qv) created the Salvation Army.

Catholics

The older religion still aroused controversy early in Victoria's reign. In 1851, dedicated Protestants marched outside the Crystal Palace at the Great Exhibition carrying placards that read 'No Popery'. Catholicism was equated with the wild, drunken Irish who built the railways and settled in ghettoes in Liverpool, Manchester and London. This had softened thirty years later into mutual tolerance; Henry Matthews became the first Catholic to join the Cabinet in 1868.

The Nonconformists

They had been called Dissenters in the seventeenth and eighteenth centuries and were despised by the establishment as rebels. The most extreme of them had gone long before Victoria's reign, to become the Bible belt of America. What was left – the Methodists, Baptists, Presbyterians etc etc – were largely urban, working class groups, often teetotal and often sullenly anti-authority.

Mammon and the Apes

All Christians, of whatever denomination, worried about the decline of organised religion. In 1851, the Church of England ran surveys on three successive Sundays in March of that year and was shocked to find that Church attendance had slipped to barely fifty per cent. The take up among Nonconformists varied from area to area – South Wales, for instance, was fiercely 'Chapel' – but the same general trend prevailed.

The simplest reason for this was the sheer workload of the working class just to survive. The coming of the machine meant *more* work, not less and a twelve hour day, six day week was the norm. Such people did not own 'Sunday best' and they had neither the time nor the inclination to attend church.

In 1860, Thomas Huxley famously took on Bishop 'Soapy Sam' Wilberforce in debates at Oxford. Huxley championed the evolutionist theories of Charles Darwin (who ducked the issue himself) that man was not created by God in His own image, from Adam and Eve, but evolved gradually from more primitive ancestors, including, somewhere along the line, the apes. Huxley wiped the floor with Wilberforce. Science could now prove that the world was not 4,000 but millions of years old. Cast doubt on one aspect of the Bible and you cast doubt on it all – the rot had set in. None of these complex arguments affected the beliefs of most people, however – even today, television programmes are littered with archaeological digs devoted to prove Noah's flood, Moses' parting of the Red Sea and other unlikely events from the Old Testament.

In Lestrade's day, whether they attended a religious service or not, men and women usually knew their hymns and prayers and never doubted for a moment that God was a kindly old gent somewhere above the clouds who was looking out for them all.

The Victorian Way of Death

Look at any Victorian photographs today and you will be struck by how dark much of the clothing is (see **Dressed to the Nines**). This is because it is probably black (all such photos are sepia today) and black was the colour of mourning.

Death was big business in Victorian England. Most people died, in the same place as they were born, at home, so death was all around in a way that it is not today. It was thought important that, however poor a man may have been in life, his exit should be as flashy as possible. Thousands of widows got themselves hopelessly in debt as a result. In 1838, an estimated £14 million was spent in this country on funerals.

Upmarket funerals were very lavish affairs. For extortionate sums, the undertaker would lay on a whole range of sable goodies to impress family and friends. Mourning cards, edged in black with designs of lilies, crying angels or weeping willows, were sent out to all and sundry with details of the funeral. The deceased, suitably dressed in his/her finest clothes, was placed in an oak/walnut/beech coffin complete with brass or silver fittings. The coffin was carried to the church/chapel and then to the grave in a black-painted hearse drawn by a pair of black horses. The whole vehicle roof was covered with black ostrich feathers.

So popular did this become that for a while the world's ostrich population was under threat. In front of the cortege and standing outside the church/chapel or family home, were the Mutes, professional mourners who never spoke, but wore black hats with streamers called 'weepers' and had their faces painted a melancholy white, often with glycerine tears down their cheeks.

The tombs themselves were astonishing examples of the stone mason's art. In London, Kensal Green, Abney Park and above all, Highgate were the modern necropolises – cities of the dead – with Egyptian Avenues, catacombs, broken columns and Celtic crosses. They were designed to be peaceful parks where a sorrowing relative or friend could sit and commune with the departed.

Everyone wore black at the funeral itself, except small children who wore white. For a year, a near relative must wear full black in public – Victoria herself took this to ridiculous extremes by wearing black for forty years after the death of her beloved Albert. After that, a certain splash of purple was permitted.

A huge debate arose in the 1870s over whether inhumation or cremation was the better way to go. Science weighed in on both sides and in the end, it was largely a matter of cost and personal preference.

By the 1890s, the fascination with death was beginning to recede. When William Gladstone (qv) had an old-fashioned plume-laden funeral in 1898, Victoria (who had never liked him anyway) was appalled. It was not only undeserved, she believed, it was anachronistic.

Was Anybody There? The Other World of Lestrade

Mesmerism, animal magnetism, a belief in life after death – whatever the forerunners of spiritualism, the Victorians embraced the idea wholeheartedly. For some, it was merely an extension of Christianity – the body might die, but the soul does not. For others, it was a genuine attempt to push back the frontiers of the unknown and to establish a new science. For yet more, it provided a comfort, a means to continue a relationship with the dear departed.

Like most things off the wall, Victorian spiritualism began in America, specifically in Hydesville, New York State, in 1848. Two sisters (how often are teenaged girls at the heart of alleged hauntings?) of the Fox family claimed to be able to communicate, by a series of raps – once for yes, twice for no – with the spirit of a drummer (travelling salesman) who had been murdered years earlier in their house. The local Press got wind of the story and the girls became first national, then international celebrities. 'Experts' of all kinds visited and tested them and it was noticed that when the girls' legs were bound tightly, there was no knocking sound, either for 'yes' or 'no'. Both girls had the genetic trait of being able to dislocate their knees at will, giving a clicking sound.*

Once their fraud had been discovered, that should have been the end of it, but the human condition being what it is, just the reverse happened. Contacting the dead took off, first in France and, by 1851, in England. That was the year that a group of Cambridge University intellectuals, led by Henry Sidgwick and his wife, set up the Ghost Club and from that, thirty years later, the Society for Psychical Research was born.

Seances became all the rage among the middle classes. Sitters arranged themselves around (ideally) oval tables and held hands. They then asked an invisible 'entity' (spirit) various questions, inviting answers as rapping sounds or by moving a wine glass around the table (telekinesis) to spell out words from pre-arranged alphabet cards. This was patented by a firm in Germany in 1904 and became known as the Ouija Board – it should, of course, have been the Ouinon or Janein board to make any sense at all.

More spectacular seances involved table-tilting – much more difficult to fabricate than raps or a moving glass – and the planchette (spirit writing). For this, a 'sensitive' or medium was required, a professional who was able to communicate with the Other Side, usually by means of a Red Indian spirit guide – presumably because they were good at tracking the trackless wastes. The medium would go into a trance and write with his/her eyes shut on a slate or paper provided. It was of course the spirit communicating with someone in the room. 'Is anybody there?' the medium

---

* The author can do something similar, if less spectacular, by pressing his toes against the sole of his shoe.

would ask and the show would begin. Exactly what was supposed to happen if the answer was 'No' is anybody's guess!

The SPR began to investigate such mediums, who, because they charged a fee for their services, were assumed to be frauds. Henry Sidgwick, Frank Podmore, F.W.H. Myers and Edmund Gurney became celebrities as 'ghost hunters'. They uncovered a variety of frauds, exposing fake spirit photographs and switching on lights in a darkened séance room as a ghost manifested itself in a sulphurous glow. Florence Cook was caught in this way with a luminous sheet over her head, emerging from a black (and therefore totally invisible) cabinet. The alabaster hands the other sitters thought were hers were still in position on the table, fingertip to fingertip. About the only medium not caught in fraudulent activity was the American Daniel Dunglass Home whose speciality was levitation. He once 'travelled' outside a New York tenement building from one room to another via the windows. There was an army of observers in both rooms and no ropes, wires or other devices could be found by any of them.

By the end of the century, despite the dogged attempts of the SPR to get to the bottom of the matter, interest in spiritualism was fading. The appalling slaughter of the First World War however saw a new fascination by a heartbroken generation. Sir Oliver Lodge and Arthur Conan Doyle (qv) believed implicitly, in the case of Doyle, falling for the puerile nonsense of the Cottingley Fairies in 1923. Two teenaged girls (no!) faked fairies at the bottom of their garden by cutting out pictures from books and taking photographs. It was early photoshop and glaringly obvious, but Doyle bought it, hook, line and sinker.

And this was the man who created Sherlock Holmes!

BRIGADE

1893
'And we leave to the streets and the workhouse the charge of the Light Brigade.'

*T*here is a new broom at Scotland Yard; Nimrod Frost. His first 'little' job for Lestrade is to investigate the reported appearance of a lion in Cornwall, a supposed savager of sheep and frightener of men. Hardly a task for an Inspector of the Criminal Investigations Department.

Yet even as Lestrade questions a witness, a man is reported dead, horrifically mauled. Having solved that case to his own satisfaction, Lestrade returns to London and to another suspicious death and then another... All old men who should have died quietly in their sleep. Is there a connection – is there a mass murderer at work?

Lestrade's superiors discount his speculations and he finds himself suspended from duty, but that is a mere technicality to the doughty Inspector. He moves from workhouse to royal palace, from backstage at the Lyceum to regimental dinner in search of clues and enlightenment.

When can his glory fade?

THE LAST OF THE
LIGHT BRIGADE

While Tennyson (qv) immortalised the charge of the Light Brigade as soon as he read William Howard Russell's dispatches in *The Times* –

> 'When can their glory fade?
> Oh, the wild charge they made!'

it was left to Rudyard Kipling (qv) to answer the question. By the time he wrote *The Last of the Light Brigade* in 1891, the world still remembered the heroism, but not the heroes –

> 'Our children's children are lisping to "honour the charge they made" –
> And we leave to the streets and the workhouse the charge of the Light Brigade!'

Kipling was using a *little* poetic licence because some of the Charge's survivors did quite well for themselves. The officers were largely landowning gentlemen anyway and their careers continued, either in or out of the army, long after October 1854. Of the Other Ranks, William Pennington of the 11th Hussars became an actor;

James Herbert of the 4th Light Dragoons ran a successful builders' merchants company; Samuel Williams of the 8th Hussars became a Beefeater at the Tower; John Linkon of the 13th Light Dragoons became, first, drill instructor to the Hampshire Yeomanry, then a man from the Pru; Edward Holland of the 17th Lancers drove a cab.

For many of them, though, service in the Crimea and in some cases India during the Mutiny of 1857 marked the end of their military lives. Some men were discharged, unfit for further duty and they had to survive as best they could.

In 1897, the journalist T.H. Roberts, publisher of *Illustrated Bits* magazine, invited all men who could prove they had ridden the Charge to watch, at his expense, the Queen's Diamond Jubilee procession as it passed along Fleet Street. Twenty-four men responded – eight of them hadn't ridden the Charge at all! There was already a Balaclava Commemoration Society which had hosted annual dinners on 25 October since 1875 and Roberts set up a fund to help needy survivors and even pay for their burial costs. Donations came from all over the world, far exceeding Kipling's 'twenty pounds and four' that his poem claimed had been donated by 'the thirty million English'. Each pensioner got a postal order every Friday, of between seven and fifteen shillings. Between 1897 and 1911, fifty-nine men received these grants, the amount running to £7,817 6s 8d. The last recipient of the fund died in September 1920 and the fund died with him.

The last survivor of the Light Brigade, Private Edwin Hughes of the 13th Light Dragoons, died on 18 May 1927, but the glory hasn't faded yet.

SOLDIERS OF THE QUEEN

Editor's note: please do not try to equate the regiments of the Victorian army with those of today. Because of cost-cutting, by all political parties, so many amalgamations have taken place that to trace a particular regiment's history is a minefield. Today's British army is smaller than at any time since 1828.

The first regular or standing army was created at the restoration of the monarchy under Charles II in 1660. Subsequent scares – Monmouth's rebellion of 1685 and the Jacobite risings of 1715 and 1745 saw further increases.

The Victorian cavalry was composed of thirty-one regiments, designated Heavy or Light (the distinction was already meaningless by 1837) which acted as the 'feelers and feeders' of the army and were ideally used to drive an already weakened enemy from the field. The huge distances involved in policing the empire meant that horses were indispensable. The oldest regiments were the Life Guards (the 'Life' in question, that of the monarch) that are still on parade today at the annual Trooping of the Colour. The newest was the 21st Hussars (later Lancers) that charged at Omdurman in 1898, along with Winston Churchill (qv). There was an inbuilt snobbery among the cavalry. They added tone to what would otherwise be a vulgar brawl.

The infantry was made up of 102 regiments and after Edward Cardwell's reforms of the 1870s, the numbered units – First Foot, Second Foot and so on – were linked to counties and recruited essentially from these areas. So the 6th Foot became the Warwickshire Regiment, the 17th the Leicestershire Regiment and the 24th, the South Wales Borderers. While the Heavy Cavalry wore scarlet uniforms and the Light, dark blue, all infantry of the line wore scarlet. The exception were the Rifle regiments, who wore dark or 'invisible' green. Scots regiments wore the kilt and other knick-knacks from over the border.

Whereas the cavalry relied on the sword or lance, the infantry weapon was the musket, replaced, as technology advanced, with the rifle.

The Artillery – Garrison, Field and Horse – used a variety of heavy guns depending on the size of the shot fired. The Horse Artillery, moving with the speed of cavalry, used nine-pounders. The Garrison Artillery, operating in siege situations, fired massive iron balls weighing 64lb. Here, too, technology constantly sought to improve ranges and killing power. The famous line by Hilaire Belloc, 'We have the Maxim gun and they have not', went a long way to explaining the British army's superiority over various colonial armies.

The auxiliary units – the Engineers, the Commissariat and Medical outfits, for example – all had their role to play and despite its shortcomings and all too frequent blinkered objection to modernisation, the British army, all bias apart, was the finest in the world.

The officer class was dominated by the gentry and aristocracy and until 1871 young gentlemen wanting a career in the cavalry or the infantry bought their rank and the promotions that followed up to the level of Lieutenant-Colonel.

This was known as the purchase system, fully approved by the Commander-in-Chief and the War Office and led to wealthy idiots like Lord Cardigan 'buying' regiments over the heads of better, but financially poorer officers. The Cardwell reforms swept this away and written examinations, preferably in the military academies of Sandhurst or Woolwich, began to establish a genuinely talented officer corps.

For the Other Ranks, the army was all too often a bolt hole. Certain minor offences could be punished by being made to join the army until the early 1960s! Wellington, regarded then as now as the country's greatest soldier, famously described the infantryman as 'the scum of the earth' and 'the sweepings of the gaols'. He did go on, however, to acknowledge that 'we have made men of them.' Recruiting sergeants or 'bringers' roamed the hiring fairs, telling tall tales of regimental glory and offering the 'Queen's shilling' as a first day's pay – the cavalry, of course, were paid more.

Life in the barracks was harsh. Flogging for minor offences did not disappear until the late 1870s and until 1871, the fixed term of service was twenty-one years. The beds were hard, in dormitories of dubious sanitation. Marriages were rare – even officers had to ask their colonel's permission – and most Other Ranks had common law wives. The phrase 'the Colonel and his lady, officers and their wives, Other Ranks and their women' was literally accurate. The children of the Other Ranks stayed with the regiment – the boys joined in the fullness of time and girls became camp followers. Not until the end of the nineteenth century did the government take any responsibility for army families, on or off army property.

Even at its grimmest, however, the army provided what civilian life could not – warm clothing, replaced every Christmas free of charge; two meals a day; and (more or less) regular pay. Not many labourer's jobs in Civvy Street could match that.

THE WORKHOUSE

To the Victorians, like any other time in the past, poverty was a pressing problem and a social evil. The Industrial Revolution, which began in Britain, transformed the economy, moved thousands from the countryside to the towns and created a brave new world. Not everybody had the acumen or the luck to benefit from this however and those who could not cope went to the wall.

One solution (and actually it was to save the government money) was to provide an alternative to the outdoor parish relief which had been operating spasmodically since 1601. Houses of Industry first made their appearance in the 1780s but in the decade that Victoria (qv) became queen, Edwin Chadwick was hired by the Poor Law Commissioners to save cash by extending the workhouse system. The New Poor Law of 1834 used the system of 'less eligibility' which meant that the workhouses were made so unpleasant that the poor would take *any* kind of dead-end, appallingly-paid job to avoid them.

Most workhouses were built in a cross formation, each arm housing a different group of the poor. Women, men, boys and girls all slept separately in these wings so that, on arrival, families were broken up. Work consisted of picking oakum (hemp, with the consistency of barbed wire) or sewing mail bags, the same 'hard labour' carried out in the prison system. The food was grim. There was a scandal at the Andover workhouse in 1846 when it was discovered that the gruel served daily contained bones with no meat content. Although this was an extreme, many other houses were little better. Meals were taken in silence. No liquor was allowed and swearing was punished by beatings. Charles Dickens exposed the workhouse in all its horror in *Oliver Twist*.

Fear of the workhouse dominated areas both urban and rural well into the twentieth century and it was not until the 1930s that they were finally closed down.

THE COUNTRY HOUSE SET

The aristocracy and gentry in Victorian England, whether old or new money, vied with each other in terms of opulence. A town house – 'town' being London, as if there was only one – was de rigeur. This served as a base from which members of the Lords and Commons occasionally visited the Houses of Parliament while their wives shopped and entertained.

The country house was an essential too and all of today's tourist attractions, whether owned by the National Trust or English Heritage, were once in private hands. Here the 'county set', Lords Lieutenant, Masters of the Hunt, JPs and landowners generally, held long weekends, especially in the 'Season' (May to September) and especially if the house was near to London.

Armies of servants ran these places, which were usually Tudor or Georgian, full of draughts and awkward rooms. The butler or steward presided over the staff with a rod of iron and under him was a strict hierarchy that ran (indoors) to the 'tweeny', the downstairs maid who lit the fires and slopped out in the basement. If the family were in town for prolonged periods or away at one of Europe's watering holes like Cannes or Spa, the place was locked and bolted, with druggets over the furniture and a skeleton staff for maintenance.

Outside, experienced woodsmen and groundskeepers tended the copse, mowed the lawn, cleared the lake and fed the deer herds. The older families had treasures galore, bought, borrowed or stolen from earlier generations, visits abroad (sometimes including conquest and the slave trade). Sporting gentlemen prided themselves on their stables, with fine thoroughbreds and joined the most prestigious Hunt they could, like the Pytchley or the Quorn. They were 'the fancy', placing bets on the outcome of horse races at Ascot and Newmarket or boxing bouts (bare knuckle before the advent of the Queensbury Rules). Their trophy rooms were full of stuffed animals, the best examples of the taxidermist's art, probably those of Rowland Ward, who mounted various exhibits shot by explorers and hunters like Samuel Baker (qv).

The ladies of these stately homes usually saw to the running of the house, deciding, with the help of Mrs Beeton's book on Domestic Management, on a daily menu, entertaining guests and working closely with the butler and staff. In many cases, they, not the master of the house, oversaw the hiring and firing. A lady's role among this class was to be an 'adornment to her sex' and to advance her husband's/son's career by being the perfect hostess, as adept in the hunting field (riding side-saddle over five-barred gates!) as she was at the three-hour dinner parties or gala balls.

The country house set still exist (just about!). The death knell of this sort of gracious living came in the 1890s when the Conservative Party (of all people!) brought in Death Duties. At a stroke, the country house became too expensive to manage and many were sold off – hence the rise of the National Trust. As democracy increased and Socialism became established by the early twentieth century, the whole dynamic of master and servant relationships changed and 'Upstairs, Downstairs' became a thing of the past, consigned to television soaps!

GORON AND THE SÛRETÉ

Each country tends to find the police force(s) of another country incomprehensible. Nowhere is this more true than France (which is a bit like L.P. Hartley's definition of the past – they do things differently there). The Sûreté, variously translated as 'safety' and 'security', was the brainchild of the thief-taker François Vidocq and was founded in 1812. It was a detective unit made up of thieves, on the grounds that it took one to catch one and smacked, to the British at least, of a private army of government spies. Despite this, it was in some ways the inspiration for Lestrade's own Detective Branch and America's FBI.

Marie-François Goron had known Lestrade for years and had a reputation as both a hard man and a brilliant detective. He investigated a number of grisly murders in France and may have been the first detective to use human hair as trace evidence in a crime (L'affaire Gouffé in 1899). He was short, fat and asthmatic, with the waxed moustache later pinched by Agatha Christie for Hercule Poirot, pince-nez and close-cropped auburn hair – 'like a rat', according to one contemporary. A.E.W. Mason, who wrote *The Four Feathers* and features in *The Giant Rat of Sumatra*, modelled his own fictional detective, Gabriel Hanaud, on Goron.

One of the most alarming features of Goron's technique was his use of torture. Suspected felons were taken to his 'cookshop' in the bowels of the Sûreté building in Paris, where their screams could not be heard.

How different from the life of our own dear policemen.

Kaiser Willie

The Emperor of Germany was later accused (wrongly) of starting the First World War. He was certainly stupid, insensitive and highly competitive but something as complex as a European war is not likely to be the work of one man.*

That man was born in January 1859 and was the eldest grandchild of Queen Victoria (qv). Because her children had the habit of marrying into European royal families, Willie was related to just about everybody. His mother was Victoria, the Princess Royal, so little Willie grew up fluent in English. His dad was Prince Frederick William of Prussia and from the age of twelve, the lad was heir to the newly-created German Empire. A bad breech birth left him with Erb's Palsy, giving him a withered left arm which was six inches shorter than the right. Look at his portraits and photos and you will see that he is usually disguising this as best he can with gloves or clutching a sword hilt. His mother taught him to ride and his grandmother to bow – he got quite proficient at both eventually.

---

*   Unless, of course, you want to blame the 19-year-old zealot, Gavrilo Princip, whose assassination of the Archduke Franz Ferdinand in Sarajevo in June 1914 triggered the whole thing.

His stupidity showed itself in 1890 when he dismissed his brilliant Chancellor, Otto von Bismarck and appointed his own lesser fry instead. He was a frequent visitor at Osborne, the Queen's home in the Isle of Wight (hence his appearance in *Brigade*) and persisted in combing his waxed moustache *upwards*, which was a gift to the cartoonists of his day.

GEE AND ESS

I have lumped these two together because they are, in a sense, the two cheeks of the same musical bum. Where would am dram be, even today, without them? There was a time, however (as in *Brigade*) when they couldn't stand the sight of each other.

William Schwenk (that is not a typo) Gilbert was born in 1836, the son of a naval surgeon. He began writing poems and plays, usually in a humorous vein and continued to do so after he met...

...Arthur Sullivan, who was born in 1842, the son of an army bandmaster. He studied at the Royal Academy of Music and at Leipzig and was considered one of the country's leading young composers.

In 1871, G&S collaborated for the first time on *Thespis*, a satire on classical drama and music. It ran for sixty-three shows as a sort of Christmas panto. *Trial by Jury* came next and it was so popular that the theatre impresarios Richard D'Oyly Carte and Carl Rosa were queuing up to book them. *The Sorcerer* wasn't great, but *HMS Pinafore* was and has such lasting appeal that it famously featured in a Simpsons television episode. Gilbert got pushier and pushier, designing sets and costumes, demanding the impossible from his cast. Sullivan and his music were pushed into the background. *The Pirates of Penzance* poked fun at grand opera even more and even had a go at the police – 'A policeman's lot is not an 'appy one' being a sentiment that Lestrade might well have shared.

The Savoy theatre opened in the 1880s, G&S's team calling themselves the Savoyards and both *Patience* and *Iolanthe* were performed in this period. *Ida*, *The Mikado* and *Ruddigore* followed, then *The Yeomen of the Guard* and *The Gondoliers*. After that, it was downhill all the way. G&S fell out, especially over production costs and they parted company. Essentially, the world of spoof opera was not big enough for both of them.

Henry Irving

Mercifully, Sir Henry Irving's acting style is not popular today. He declaimed rather than spoke his lines (usually Shakespeare) and had the irritating habit of dragging one foot behind him on stage. In one respect, however, he was very modern. Realizing that John Henry Brodribb would get nowhere as a thesp, he changed his name to Irving and the rest is history. He is widely reckoned to be a model for Stoker's Dracula and somebody else took that further in the 1950s when 'tall, dark and gruesome'; Christopher Lee got the role of the Count in the Hammer films.

Irving came from a working class family in Somerset and worked as a clerk briefly before taking to the London stage. He slowly built up a following at the Lyceum Theatre, the Haymarket and the Gaiety. He was Richard III, he was Hamlet, he was Dr Faustus and Macbeth. He was the first of the theatrical knights.

Bram Stoker

They say everyone has a book in them and in the case of Abraham Stoker, that book was *Dracula*. He features in the Lestrade series as the theatrical agent of Henry Irving (qv) and before that he had been a civil servant. It was the 1897 novel about the Undead that made his name, however.

Born in Clontarf in 1847, he changed from a sickly, bed-ridden child to a 'jock' at Trinity College, Dublin, winning athletics prizes galore. He knew Oscar Wilde (qv) and, through Irving, anybody who was anybody among the luvvies of the day.

When he met Lestrade, he had not yet written his most famous book but he had holidayed in Whitby, where part of the story is set and was a keen student of Eastern European folklore.

Daisy Warwick

Frances Evelyn Grenville was one of the ladies with whom Lestrade had a fling (give the guy a break – he put his life on the line often enough in the course of his career). She was seven years his junior and her mother was descended from Nell Gwynne, orange seller to King Charles II (which might explain why 'Daisy' established colleges, in later life, for women in agriculture).

She married Lord Brooke in 1881 and when he became the Earl of Warwick, she moved to the magnificent castle now owned by Madame Tussauds. A celebrated hostess, she knew everybody and had affairs with a variety of wealthy and important men – and one poor and not very important one.

According to some sources, she helped fund (though she was constantly in debt) the chapel of the current writer's school in Warwick, known as Daisy's Pulpit.*

According to other sources, the music hall song 'Daisy, Daisy' was based on her. No doubt she looked very sweet on a bicycle.

---

* This piece of information has come as a total surprise to the author, who would have been rather fonder of chapel services had he only known, back in the day.

The Dead Man's Hand

1895
'There was no 9.38 from Penge.'

Anon.

*T*he London Underground Railway, in 1895, was described as 'dark, deadly and halfway to Hell'. Only too true, for as the last train rattled into Liverpool Street, the one remaining passenger did not get off. How could she, when her eyes stared sightless and her heart had stopped?

There was another corpse at the Elephant in the morning, wedged between the seats like an old suitcase. And another had missed the late-night connection at Stockwell. What was left of her lay on the floor of the 'padded cell', her shoes kicked off in the lashings of her agony as she died.

There is a maniac at large and Inspector Lestrade is detailed to work with the Railway Police, something he needs a little less than vivisection. Heedless of warnings to 'mind the gap' and 'mind the doors', the doughty detective plunges through a tangled web of vicious deviants to solve a string of murders so heinous that every woman in London goes in fear of her life.

Who is the legendary Blackfriars Dan? What are the secrets of the Seven Sisters? Whose body lies at Ealing? Will the London Transport System survive, or will Lestrade run out of steam?

The Underground Railway

The Underground or Tube began with the Metropolitan Railway that opened in 1863 when men still wore tall stove-pipe hats and a lady would not be seen dead without a crinoline. The line ran from Paddington to Farringdon on the Great Western's broad 7 foot gauge, using wooden carriages lit by gas and locomotives powered by steam. 38,000 people were carried on the first day and the venture never looked back. The District Railway opened in 1868 from South Kensington to Westminster and the 'circle line' was completed by 1884. The first deep level lines, with 10ft 2in tunnels, opened in 1890 with electric locomotives. This was the 'twopenny tube'.

Lifts were dodgy; there were no escalators until 1911 and there was the constant problem of over-heating and lack of ventilation. The engineering necessary to build the tunnels, avoiding the Thames and the extensive sewerage system, was phenomenal, bringing the finest technical expertise to the fore along with the guts and sheer hard work of the men at the rock face.

Trains themselves were notorious places for crime of all sorts. Ladies felt unsafe travelling with men who were, of course, all beasts and in the 'padded cells' – the nickname for the carriages – a girl could find herself horribly isolated. Some travelled (allegedly) with hat pins in their mouths to dissuade beasts from kissing them. The Railway Police was formed out of the regular forces to deal with such crime, including the use of plainclothesmen (see **Watching the Detectives**) to trap the less-than-careful criminal.

The Empire on which the sun never sets

It is a remarkable fact, as the Victorians never tired of saying, that one of the smallest islands in the world should become the mother country of the biggest empire in history.

It used to be said that trade follows the flag; that is military conquest took place and the money men moved in. In fact, it was usually the opposite. The Hudson's Bay Company, the East India Company, the West India Company and dozens of others, saw the vast potential of the undiscovered – and unexploited – world and moved in. They then had to be protected, from natives and rivals alike, by the army and navy.

The fictional Sleigh brothers in *The Dead Man's Hand* came from all over when a crisis threatens the family, so for the sake of this book, I have focused on the areas of empire where they are based.

India – 'the brightest jewel in the crown'
Colonized by the East India Company as early as 1600, India became at once a land of magic, untold riches and controversy. The Company set up 'factories' (trading posts) at Bombay, Calcutta and Madras, exporting spices, silk and tea. The French had similar ideas with their Compagnie des Indes and the eighteenth century saw a series of colonial

wars in which, by 1800, Britain was the winner. By a combination of diplomacy and old-fashioned military invasion, by the time Lestrade was born, all India was under direct or indirect British rule. After the Mutiny of 1857 – which was, in fact, an army revolt, not the beginnings of an independence movement – things settled down considerably. From long before 1877, when Disraeli (qv) suggested that the Queen (qv), God bless her, be given the title of the Empress of India, the British government ruled India direct in what was known as the Raj. British regiments served for years in India and the first generation of such men took Indian women as their wives. Indian words became part of the English language – doolally explained the odd behaviour of men disembarking in the unhealthy climate at Deolali; the 'mem' referred to an officer's wife, *memsahib* in Urdu; the officer himself was *sahib*, lord. The game of polo was first played in India, by the 10th Hussars in 1869 and a whole range of bizarre foodstuffs found their way to British dining tables.

There was no move to Christianise the Hindus, Sikhs or Muslims of India, despite constant rumours to the contrary and British law, education and the English language left their mark on the sub-continent. Only on the North-West Frontier with Russian-haunted Afghanistan was there constant tension, with two major campaigns in Lestrade's lifetime.

Australia – Down Under

James Cook is responsible for Australia. It and New Zealand were always rather afterthoughts in the colonial scheme of things. The odd truth is that Britain did not actually have an imperial policy until the 1870s when Disraeli (qv) made it synonymous with the Tory Party. The empire grew almost by accident; no one in Whitehall ever sat down and said, 'Right. Which bits of the world do we want to grab?' – essentially, Adolf Hitler's policy in the 1930s. America, Canada and India always came first – the Antipodes were a sort of PS. Even though Australia provided sheep and wool and New Zealand dairy products, the bald fact is that so much of Australia is uninhabitable means that it was always going to be an economic white elephant. Everybody's eyes lit up in 1851 when gold was discovered, but it was all a storm in a teacup.

The impact of Australia on Britain was negligible in Lestrade's day. Their lighthorsemen provided a splash of colour at various royal jubilees but that was about all. After we stopped sending our convicts to Botany Bay (1837) some people questioned what was the point of Australia at all.

Africa – the Dark Continent

One of the last places in the world to be discovered, explored and mapped, central Africa held a romantic mysticism like nowhere else. The Romans had settled across the northern coast and the Dutch, the Portuguese and the British had toe holds in the south. But what lay at the heart of Africa was anybody's guess and it led to rumours like the mythical immortal Prester John of Ethiopia who was a Christian king ruling beyond the Mountains of the Moon. Ivory from the Serengeti, shooting safaris by white hunters, the diamonds of Kimberley, all this was bound inextricably with legends of King Solomon's buried treasure and men with their faces in their chests.

From the 1880s onwards, most European countries got involved in the 'scramble for Africa'. It seemed particularly greedy of Britain and France to want yet more land for themselves, but other countries had something to prove.

Germany in particular was a new country after 1871, desperate to build an empire quickly. They all exploited the native populations. Sir Bartle Frere, an incredibly pushy civil servant, forced a war with the Zulu in 1879. Between them, King Leopold of the Belgians and Cecil Rhodes worked thousands of Africans to death.

On the plus side, we ended slavery in the Sudan and brought medicine, schools and roads to a dangerous wilderness. David Livingstone brought God, Richard Burton, John Hanning Speke and Samuel Baker (qv) brought the Royal Geographical Society.

Today, imperialism is a dirty word. There have been recent moves by bigoted, badly educated university students, for example, to wipe Cecil Rhodes from the history books. Yes, there was exploitation, yes, there was cruelty, racism and arrogance. But there was also Christianity, love, care and thought. Those things made the empire great and millions of people benefitted as a result. If you think I exaggerate, just reflect on this. Were it not for the British empire, there might well still be slaves in Sudan and thousands of widows in India would still be expected to throw themselves onto the blazing funeral pyres of their dead husbands.

Edward Marshall Hall

'Oh yes, he's the great defender de doo de doo,' as the Platters nearly sang in 1955. He loomed over the court rooms in Victorian and Edwardian London, known for his brilliant oratory and histrionics, a Perry Mason before his time.

Like virtually all lawyers of his day, Marshall Hall was educated at public school (Rugby) and 'Oxbridge' (St John's, Cambridge) before being called to the Bar. Famous for playing to the gallery (in fact, the jury) he turned his mournful gaze on the twelve men and true in defence of a murderous prostitute in 1894 – 'Look at her, gentlemen... God never gave her a chance – won't you?'

He would encounter Lestrade several times during their careers, defending the ghastly Frederick Seddon, the revolting George Joseph Smith and the almost wholly innocent Harvey Hawley Crippen – in fact, he turned Crippen down at the last moment.

One thing about Marshall Hall is certain – they don't make barristers like him any more.

H.G. WELLS

As Lestrade was investigating the murders in *The Dead Man's Hand*, Herbert George Wells was writing *The Time Machine*. The man who has been called the 'father of science fiction' was born in Bromley, Kent, in September 1866. He broke his leg when he was eight and the weeks in bed turned him into a voracious reader. The lower middle class Wells family were usually strapped for cash and H.G. worked as a draper's assistant which gave him the inspiration for *Kipps* years later.

He won a scholarship to the Normal School of Science (now Imperial College, London) with an income of 21s a week (which could keep many working class families from the breadline). By 1890, Wells had obtained a B.Sc. in zoology, went on to teach – among others, the Winnie the Pooh creator, A.A. Milne – and to write biology textbooks.

A universal man, H.G. wrote 'realism' novels, science fiction and short stories and wasn't a bad artist. His other abiding interest, however, was women. He married his cousin, Isabel, in 1891 but fell for – and moved in with – one of his students three years later. A lot of other ladies, including the Russian spy Moura Budberg, followed.

His influence was enormous but not everybody was impressed. In the 1930s, G.K. Chesterton (qv) wrote, 'Mr Wells is a born storyteller who has sold his birthright for a pot of message.'

AUBREY BEARDSLEY

'Grotesque', 'decadent', 'erotic' – all three words have been used to describe Beardsley's art; and a couple of them to describe the artist himself.

Aubrey Beardsley was born in Brighton in 1872 and became a musical prodigy at his local grammar school. His first drawings appeared in the school magazine. Bored working as a clerk, he took up art professionally and visited Paris, pinching the style of Toulouse-Lautrec and the trend for *Japonnais*, oriental art. He co-founded the *Yellow Book*, illustrating it with his distinctive style of black and white surrealism. The Stomach Dance, the Peacock Skirt and various depictions of Salome are typical of this period, but as well as illustrating classical works like Morte d'Arthur, Beardsley produced political satirical sketches too.

Oscar Wilde (qv) described him as having 'a face like a silver hatchet and grass green hair'. He was a fastidious dresser and his sexuality is still up for grabs, as it were. He possibly had a relationship with his sister, but equally he could have been asexual. He became a Catholic in 1897 and, plagued by tuberculosis as he had been all his life, he died in France the following year.

W.G. Grace

William Gilbert Grace was *the* Victorian/Edwardian cricketer par excellence. In the heady days when all cricketers wore white, nobody needed body armour or was afraid of the ball, Grace was the perfect gentleman, bringing a civilised game to the unenlightened nations of the world. From 1865 to 1908 he was captain of England, Gloucestershire, the Gentlemen, Marylebone Cricket Club and many more. He was a batsman, bowler and fielder without peer; he was also a doctor of medicine and enjoyed a considerable amount of gamesmanship as a result of his highly competitive nature.

Despite never going to university – both Oxford and Cambridge tried to win him over for his cricketing prowess – he opted for Bristol Medical School instead. In 1873 he became the first to achieve a 'double' – 1,000 runs and 100 wickets in a single season.

Eventually giving up as the years took their toll, Grace said he had no choice as 'the ground was getting a bit too far away'.

The Demon Drink

Alcoholic beverages were not new in Victorian England but the reformers of that period saw drunkenness as a vicious social evil. Gin was traditionally referred to as 'Mother's Ruin' but all alcohol had destructive qualities, according to some. When Henry Mayhew wrote his monumental *London Labour and the London Poor* in 1851, the drunkenness of the working class was endemic and the cause of persistent, casual violence. Men who got their wages daily or weekly spent some – or all – of it in the local pub. If they were violent drunks, they would stagger home and beat seven bells out of their wives and children. Look again at the victims of Jack the Ripper – they all drank for England and at least three of them were under the influence, not to say paralytic, when he struck.

Various Acts of Parliament had tried to limit the licencing hours and the gallons of alcohol consumed but this was a losing battle. Gladstone (qv) believed that he lost the election of 1874 because of his Licensing Act of two years earlier. 'We have been borne down,' he said, 'in a torrent of gin and beer.' Neither the powerful breweries – there were dozens of them in Victorian England – nor the average drinking man who by now was actually or potentially a voter, was prepared to have their profits and pleasures curtailed.

Into the breach stepped a variety of Temperance Societies. The armed forces had their own. The son of the brewing dynasty, the Charringtons, had his, giving out badges with the logo 'The Blue Ring of Total Abstinence' to the saved. Methodists, Baptists, Rechabites and Welsh and Scots Nonconformists without number fought to create 'dry' boroughs and counties, where no liquor at all was available on Sundays. The tourist pioneer Thomas Cook set up his railway deal for teetotal Midlanders as early as 1841.

Inevitably, women were seen as the victims of drunkenness because it was assumed (wrongly) that only men drank. So feminism took centre ground as many of the Temperance groups were female-led. Marching with placards screaming 'Down with Demon Drink', they wrote articles in parish magazines and inveigled the great and the good to denounce the evils of liquor. While men were perhaps perfectly happy to read the teetotal views of the Archbishop of Canterbury and the Commissary-General, they were probably less impressed with the thirst-quenching alternatives after a hard day in the fields or the factory that such publications suggested. They were usually made from nettles and tasted disgusting.

THE GUARDIAN ANGEL

1897/8
'And a naughty boy was he...'

*H*e was in his forty-third year and knee-deep in murder. Well, what was new? Sholto Lestrade wouldn't really have it any other way.

The first fatality in a series of killings which was to become the most bizarre in the celebrated Inspector's career, was a captain of the 2nd Life Guards, found battered over the head in the Thames at Shadwell Stair, an Ashanti War medal wedged between his teeth. Lestrade's next summons was to the underground caves of Wookey Hole where the demise of an Egyptologist – a scarab clamped between his molars – prompted the question; can a man dead for a thousand years reach beyond the grave and commit murder?

The further death from a cadaveric spasm of an enobled young subaltern whilst on picquet duty (this time a locket is his dying mouthful) forces Lestrade to impersonate 'Lt Lister, Duke of Lancaster's Own Yeomanry' and into becoming a barrack-room lawyer of incisive command.

As the body count rapidly rises, Lestrade, constantly and relievedly touching base with his 'family', Harry and Letitia Bandicoot of the Hall, Huish Epsicopi, varies a volatile lifestyle with dinner at Blenheim Palace; a disastrous cycle tour ending in a night in gaol;

a near-fatal trip in an air balloon; and masterful mediation in East End gang warfare on the Ratcliffe Highway.

Eventually, some seven cadavers later, things begin to fit into place and the final conundrum emerges; who or what is Coquette Perameles?

VICTORIA'S SMALL WARS

The 'big war' of Queen Victoria's reign was the Crimea (1854-6), involving Britain, France and Turkey on the one hand and the beastly Russians on the other. After that, Britain used diplomacy in Europe and only went to war with various enterprises to protect/safeguard/extend the Empire, depending on your point of view.

In the Colonies, the 'thin red line' – the original is actually the 'thin red streak' of William Howard Russell of *The Times* – became the thin khaki line as that colour replaced the scarlet of British infantry as early as 1857 in India. The clashes that occurred usually saw the British outnumbered, but superior technology, especially firepower, was more than a balance for that. The sheer dogged heroism was summed up by Rudyard Kipling's (qv) poem *The Gentlemen in Khaki*, as drawn by Richard Caton Woodville in 1899. Copies of this, a hatless 'Tommy' with bandaged head and fixed bayonet, were reproduced on ladies' fans, table centrepieces and trivets for the kitchen.

There were numerous campaigns in India, but easily the most determined and difficult enemy were the Sikhs with their steel throwing quoits and deadly artillery. At the height of the Indian Mutiny (1857), mutineers were tied to cannon mouths and blown apart in reprisal for their slaughter of women and children in Cawnpore.

In Africa, war was waged against tribal kingdoms – Prempeh of the Ashanti (1874), Cetewayo of the Zulu (1879) – all ending in the same way; victory for the British and extension of the empire. There were some bloody reversals on the way however, especially Isandlwhana (January 1879) when the 24th Foot were all but wiped out before the heroic defence of Rorke's Drift a day later which resulted in a record bestowal of eleven Victoria Crosses.

Some of the most famous men of Lestrade's day made their names in colonial conflict. Henry Havelock was the hero of Lucknow in the Indian Mutiny; Charles Gordon cleared the Sudan of slavery before his death at the hands of the 'mad' Mahdi; Robert Napier was imperious at Magdala in Abyssinia; Frederick Roberts became 'Bobs of Kandahar', knocking seven bells out of the Afghans.

For others, things did not go so well. Redvers Buller was exposed as one of the most inept generals in history in the Boer war; Lord Chelmsford made a hash of things against the Zulu; and Lord Kitchener had to wait until the First World War to find his own particular level of incompetence.

Today's chattering classes by and large find the Empire and all it stood for distasteful; to them, Victoria's small wars are little more than exercises in destruction. That is not how it was at the time.

'ALL SIR GARNET'

You don't hear phrases like that any more! It meant 'all's in order, everything's all right' which is a clue to the reliability of Garnet Joseph Wolseley KP, GCB, DM, GCMG, VD [surely not?] PC [well, I never!]. He was born into the army, the son of a major in the 25th Foot, in 1833. He joined the regiment without purchase in 1852 on account of his father's position. He served in several regiments in the 1850s, was wounded but reached the rank of captain by the time the Crimean War was underway. He lost an eye serving with the Royal Engineers in the siege of Sebastopol and was put in the thick of things again in the Indian Mutiny of 1857.

He became a hero having relieved the siege of Lucknow, was mentioned in despatches and given the rank of substantive major by 1861.

In Canada later that year, Wolseley took himself off to investigate the American civil war, then underway, working with the Confederate generals Robert E. Lee, 'Stonewall' Jackson and James Longstreet. He wrote a treatise on the cavalry officer, Nathan Bedford Forrest, who went on to form the Ku Klux Klan after the war.

The Ashanti campaign (1874) which features in the *Guardian Angel* made Wolseley a household name. Loaded with cash and honours, he became a Major-General in 1877 and the model for the Major-General in Gilbert and Sullivan's (qv) *The Pirates of Penzance*. The pith helmets worn by all troops in hot climates were known as the Wolseley pattern.

Lady Randolph Churchill

However you look at her, Jenny Jerome was a stunner. She was almost exactly Lestrade's age, born in Brooklyn in 1854, the child of financier Leonard Jerome. She was a brilliant pianist – a skill expected of daughters of the rich – and worked – which was not expected – as a magazine editor.

In August 1873 she attended Cowes sailing regatta in the Isle of Wight – where anybody who was anybody could be found in boaters and striped blazers – and met Lord Randolph (pronounced Randofe) Churchill. The cottage where he proposed is still there along the waterfront – it used to belong to Lord Cardigan of Light Brigade fame. After endless family wranglings over the financial side of the settlement, the couple married in April 1874 at the British Embassy in Paris (Jenny's second home).

Winston (qv) was born eight months later (tut! tut!) and much of what we know about her comes from his autobiography *My Early Life*. He adored her – 'she shone like the evening star' – but the wife of an aristocrat and busy politician had to leave her sons' upbringing to a variety of nannies and preparatory schools.

Jenny was bright, vivacious, funny and a flirt; all of which made her popular at society bashes. When Lord Randolph died, probably of syphilis, in 1895, Jenny was much in demand. Though constantly broke, she went through men like a knife through butter and it was in this hectic whirl of socialising that she met Lestrade in the summer of 1897, via her friend, Lady Daisy Warwick.

PHEW! IT'S A SCORCHER!
LES BICYCLETTES DE BELSIZE –
AND EVERYWHERE ELSE!

They have always been louts. Now, they wear Lycra; then, they wore deerstalkers and plus fours. The cycling craze hit Britain in the 1880s spearheaded by the Bicycle Touring Club founded in 1878. There was even a National Cyclists' Union, established at the same time, which put up signs to warn cyclists of dangerous bends and other hazards.

It was all the fault of blacksmith Kirkpatrick MacMillan, of Courthill, near Dumfries, who invented the 'velocipede' in 1839, a gadget with levers and cranks that would develop into the bicycle proper. It was Rowley Turner, who, in his spare time from working for the Coventry Sewing Machine Company, bought a Michaux velocipede from France and popularised it. The phenomenon took off with the introduction of pedals and brakes (not all bikes had the latter in Lestrade's day) and a number of different types were on the market. The Facile was supposed to be the easiest to ride but elderly gentlemen preferred the Penny Farthing, so called from the differing size of the wheels.

Clubs proliferated all over the country, allowing men and women (often together – shock! horror!) the freedom of what, in the 1880s, was still the open road. 'There has not been,' said Lord Balfour, 'a more civilising invention in the memory of the present generation... than [that] of the bicycle' – but that was Lord Balfour, and what did he know?

Dangerous tearaways who hurtled through crowded streets were called 'scorchers' and the police took a particularly dim view of them.

The Hallowed House

1901
'Quid omnes tangit, ab omnibus approbetur.'*
Edward I

*B**ritain has entered the twentieth century. Queen Victoria is dead and the Boer War rages on. Inspector Lestrade is called upon to investigate the brutal death of Ralph Childers, MP. It is but the first in a series of bizarre and perplexing murders that lead Lestrade around the country in pursuit of his enquiries.*

The connection between the victims appears to be politics. Is someone trying to destroy the government? It would seem so, particularly when a bomb is found in the Palace of Westminster. But who is responsible? The Fenians? Or have the Suffragettes decided upon a more drastic course of action to further their cause?

During his investigations, Lestrade encounters some old and some new faces. Amongst the new ones are the brother and cousin of the late Sherlock Holmes who died eleven years ago at the Reichenbach Falls. But is Holmes really dead? Dr Watson doesn't think so. Someone wants to keep Holmes alive and Lestrade is forced to tread the boards (playing himself) to discover the truth. And, as if things aren't serious enough, the King is kidnapped just before his coronation.

Amidst all this, Lestrade is faced with the knowledge that his daughter is growing up not knowing who her real father is.

---

*   Look it up on Google – do I have to do everything for you?

Politics

No, don't skip this bit – it's quite interesting!

The running of the country was almost exclusively in male hands. Not until the 1860s could women become involved in local government and not until 1919, by which time Lestrade was on the verge of retirement, were they given the vote. The majority of both Commons and Lords were the product of the public schools and many of them followed their fathers in the business of government, either by standing for parliament or inheriting a title.

In theory, the monarch was at the helm, the only woman in the business. Victoria (qv) took the job of government seriously, but relied heavily on her statesmen (except Gladstone (qv), whom she loathed) for key decisions. She hated the female suffrage movement and did nothing whatsoever for the cause of feminism. In 1884, she became the last monarch to veto a bill – Henry Labouchere's Criminal Law Amendment Act. This was supposed to clean up Britain's moral act by introducing harsh measures against homosexuals. When Labouchere tried to include lesbians in this, Victoria told him that there was no such thing and that part of the Bill vanished without trace.

Until 1911, the Lords were the senior house, throwing their unelected weight around and interfering in various Commons' moves. In that year, in a constitutional punch-up, the Lords lost their power to veto or even to delay financial Bills and they've been fighting a rearguard action ever since.

The Commons represented the small, entirely male electorate throughout the nineteenth century. Reform Acts in 1832, 1867 and 1884 extended the electorate so that the number of voters increased. Even so, the right to vote was based on the ownership of property so it was not until 1919 that the principle of universal male suffrage was achieved.

For much of Lestrade's life there were only two parties. The Tories, who styled themselves Conservatives from the 1840s, represented the rural, agricultural way of life in old England. The Whigs, who became the Liberals in 1859, were more radical and had more regard for the modernity of Britain, with its rapid industrialisation and the growth of cities. This is an over-simplification. Party politics, then as now, was not merely about principles and attitudes; it was about getting one over on the Opposition. So Disraeli (qv), who, as leader of the Conservatives in the Commons, shouldn't have approved of even yet more middle-class voters, nevertheless brought in the 1867 Reform Act which not only achieved this but stole Gladstone's thunder in the process.

In foreign policy, there was a similar fuzziness. The Conservatives were the party of Empire, waving the flag and sending the gunboat. The Liberals were far more humanitarian, but it depended on the issue. Gladstone defended the 'noble savage', the Zulu, when Disraeli's government went to war with them in 1879. When the Turks attacked Christians in their own empire, however, Gladstone demanded that Disraeli declare war and that the Turks should be 'kicked out of Europe bag and baggage'.

Behind parliament (for which, then as now, there was no intelligence test) stood a vast, apolitical Civil Service. There was an appallingly amateur atmosphere to all this until Gladstone brought in much-needed reform in 1872. From then on, all Civil Service posts had to be applied for and written examinations taken. Even here, however, there was an exception – the Foreign Office remained untouched!

Despite the casual attitudes of large numbers of men involved at all levels of government, the nineteenth century saw a vast raft of legislation, from the ages of children allowed to work in factories, to the number of water troughs provided for draught horses. By the 1880s, England was 'paved, gassed and watered' in a way that had never been seen before and was the envy of the modern world.

From 1848 onwards, the 'spectre of Communism' spread across the world. Karl Marx and Friedrich Engels wrote *The Communist Manifesto* in England but it was not until the 1880s that an English translation appeared. Neither Conservative nor Liberal genuinely spoke for the working man and so, in that decade, Socialism was born. In parliament, it became the Independent Labour Party in 1892, its first MP the Scottish miners' leader, James Keir Hardie. He outraged other Members by turning up at the Commons in a deerstalker, as opposed to a silk top hat *and* he was accompanied by a brass band! For many Victorians, civilization had come to an end.

'Good Old Winnie'

Winston Churchill pops up so often in the Lestrade sagas that he should almost appear in one of the standalone sections of this book. He was born at the end of November 1874 to Lord Randolph Churchill, son of the 7th Duke of Marlborough and the American heiress Jenny Jerome (qv). Since his parents were so busy and in constant demand among the county set, Winston was brought up largely by his nanny, Elizabeth Everest, whom he called Womany. A rebellious and lazy child, he didn't excel at school, famously writing nothing but his name in his entrance exam to Harrow. He got in because of his dad.

A plain, ginger boy with a lisp and a slight stammer, he didn't have much going for him. Good at History and Maths, he wanted to follow his father into politics, but Randolph was not impressed with the boy, barely knew him and he died of syphilis when Winston was twenty. By that time, he had become a cadet at Sandhurst, met Lestrade (in *Brigade*) and joined the 4th Hussars as a subaltern. That brought him £300 a year but he was constantly broke and had to visit the bank of Mama on more than one occasion.

He served in Cuba and India, damaging an arm but becoming a useful polo player. His writing ability was considerable and he wrote articles for the dailies and *The River War*, an account of his exploits in the Sudan in 1898, where he famously charged with the 21st Lancers. While toying with politics (he failed to get in at Oldham in July of 1899) he went as a war correspondent for the *Morning Post* to cover the Boer War. Here, on an armoured train, he was captured by the Boers and escaped, turning himself into an international hero. This time, Oldham welcomed him with open arms and his political career was under way.

In the Commons, Churchill dithered between the Conservatives (his father's party) and the Liberals, especially influenced by the mercurial 'Welsh wizard' David Lloyd George, who, contrary to rumour, did not know Lestrade's father. He became heavily involved in the Liberal Reforms of the People's Budget, setting up Labour Exchanges (today's Jobcentres) and creating Old Age Pensions. On the negative side, he supported eugenics (sterilising the mentally impaired) and, as Home Secretary, ordered troops into South Wales against the striking miners of Tonypandy.

Lestrade met him again in the Siege of Sidney Street (*Leviathan*) when a gang of anarchists holed up in a house at Number 100. There was no actual reason why Churchill should have been there (he was Home Secretary at the time), but he always enjoyed excitement and once again ordered in the big guns – a howitzer in fact.

He was First Lord of the Admiralty by 1911 and stayed in that post (amazingly) until he fouled the anchor somewhat with the ill-conceived Gallipoli campaign of 1915. A maverick, loathed and loved in equal proportion, he was out of office until 1939, as the clock wound down to his 'finest hour'.

JAMES KEIR HARDIE

A hero of the Left, James Keir Hardie was born in in 1856 and brought up by his ship's carpenter stepfather and his housemaid mother in Lanarkshire. Working from the age of seven as a messenger boy, his education was erratic to say the least and he took any kind of menial work to survive.

Destined for a (short) career as a coal miner, then one of the most dangerous jobs in the world, Keir, as he was known, got religion, joined a Temperance society (see **The Demon Drink**) and his natural skill at public speaking made him a local miners' leader. By 1879, he was National Secretary of the Scottish miners and he organised a wave of strikes to secure better pay. He also ran a soup kitchen from his home, helped by his new wife.

To make ends meet in desperate times, Hardie took to journalism and joined the Liberal Association. It became obvious to intelligent men like him that Gladstone's (qv) Liberals were not the party for the people, so he gravitated to the new Independent Labour Party (ILP) and became the member for West Ham in 1892. Famously, he turned up at the Commons in a plain tweed suit, red tie and deerstalker, which was wrongly described by the Right Wing press as a working man's 'cloth cap'.

He became an anti-establishment rebel, spookily predicting the fraught future of the later Edward VIII when he was very young – '… this boy will be surrounded by sycophants and flatterers by the score… A line will be drawn between him and the people whom he is to be called upon some day to reign over.' How right he was.

The Forgotten Prime Minister – Andrew Bonar Law

W^{ho?}

'Votes for Women!' – the Suffragettes

Lestrade has a love-hate relationship with the Suffragettes. He fell in love with one of them (Emily Greenbush) but is equally to be seen facing them in a police cordon against their battle lines.

It was rather ironic that the most powerful woman in the world, Queen Victoria (qv) (God Bless Her) did nothing to back the cause of female emancipation. In fact, she once wrote in her diary that such women should be horse-whipped. Female voting was allowed in municipal corporations from 1869 but the agitation for a general franchise took far longer. John Stuart Mill was almost a lone voice in the all-male parliament at the time trying to put the case. Similar demands around the world met with varying success. The women of Wyoming could vote in their state legislation from 1869, but the Swiss (astonishingly) did not see the light until 1972.

The first society for female emancipation was formed in Sheffield in 1857 and it became national ten years later. Hampered by society's views of female behaviour, the cause achieved virtually nothing until 1903 when Emmeline Pankhurst came to lead the Women's Social and Political

Union (WSPU). With the Liberals in power in the early years of the twentieth century, the Suffragettes (a deliberately sexist term coined by the *Daily Mail*) hoped to win through and took to the streets. They wore white, green and purple as their colours, carried banners and went on marches. They wrote letters to newspapers and harangued politicians at all levels.

Most men responded badly, throwing them out of public meetings and sending for the police. The Pankhursts' followers chose gaol rather than a fine for public disorder because it gave them more publicity. They padlocked themselves to the railings outside No. 10, Downing Street. They yelled their demands from boats on the Thames passing the MPs taking tea on the terrace of the Houses of Parliament. They set fire to letter boxes, carried bricks in their handbags and wrestled with policemen. Men in turn were delighted to take them on, proudly displaying hair ripped from Suffragettes' heads in their button-holes like 'Red Indian' scalps.

Enlightened liberals like Winston Churchill (qv) and Edward Grey detested them, but it was Lloyd George who came in for most of their wrath. The Suffragettes bombed his house. Spectacularly, in 1913, Emily Davison threw herself under the hoofs of the king's horse at the Derby of that year (but see *Lestrade and the Devil's Own* for what *really* happened). The government's response was the notorious 'Cat and Mouse' Act of the same year, when female prisoners on hunger strike were force fed and released, only to be re-arrested once their health was restored.

Ironically, it was not the Suffragettes but the First World War (qv) which won women the vote. The WSPU shut down its activities from 1914 as part of the war effort and thousands of women took the place of men on the farms and in the munitions factories. A grateful government rewarded them with the vote in 1919, although only for those over thirty; it was assumed that by then, most of them would be married and would do as their husbands told them!

As we would say today – 'Yeah! Right!'

Rudyard Kipling

Joseph Rudyard Kipling is today often dismissed by the Bright Young Things as 'the poet of Empire' and therefore a racist. His *White Man's Burden* is cited as typical of his Anglo-Saxon superior stance. In fact, the poem is about the Americans in the Philippines and has nothing to do with *British* Imperialism at all.

He was born in India in 1865 only eight years after the Indian Mutiny (or Sepoy War as it should properly be called) rocked Britain's confidence in the government of India. For the first years of his life he lived in Bombay and then, as was usual at the time, was sent to boarding school in England.

He was a journalist, virtually created the short story and his poem *If* is probably the most quoted in the world as a superb piece of warm-hearted advice from father to son. Kipling's own son, Jack, was killed while serving with the Irish Guards on the Western Front in the First World War and the poet never got over it – 'Have you news of my boy Jack? *Not this tide...*' – is heartbreaking.

He was the creator of the magical Mowgli characters in the *Jungle Book* and more than anyone else, spoke for the common soldier, the type of man he met by the hundreds while working in India as an adult. Those who accuse Kipling of racism would do well to remember the last lines of *Gunga Din* – 'Though I've belted you and flayed you, by the living Gawd that made you, you're a better man than I am, Gunga Din.'

He also had a wonderfully romantic concept of English history, marching with the Roman legions, marauding with the Saxons, sailing with the Armada. His humour twinkles in the *Just So Stories* and he won the Nobel Prize for Literature in 1907.

Lestrade met 'Gigger' as his friends called him because of his short-sightedness, in rather unfortunate circumstances on the South Downs, near the writer's home at Batemans. They got on like a house on fire.

The Gift of the Prince

1903
'Lang may your lum reek, Lestrade.'

Sholto Lestrade had never smelt the tangle o' the Isles before Arthur, Duke of Connaught put him on the trail to the Highlands. Murder is afoot among the footmen on the Royal Household; a servant girl, Amy Macpherson, has been brutally murdered.

Ineptly disguised as a schoolmaster in his bowler and Donegal, with his battered old Gladstone, the intrepid Superintendent is impelled by a villainous web of conspiracy northwards to the Isle of Skye by way of Balmoral.

With the skirl of the pipes in his ears and more than a dram of a certain medicinal compound inside him, Lestrade, following the most baffling clues he has yet unravelled, takes the low road alone, save for the trusty yet mysterious Alistair Sphagnum in his twin-engined, bright red boneshaker. Narrowly escaping the inferno of Room 13 in the North British Hotel, Lestrade falls foul of The McNab of That Ilk and The Mackinnon of That Ilk and plays a very odd game of 'Find the Lady' in Glamis Castle.

Coming from Scotland Yard is no help at all to a Sassenach in trews and everyone is convinced it's a job for the Leith Police. Threatened by ghoulies, ghosties and wee, sleekit beasties, Lestrade hears things go bump in the night before solving the case of Drambuie.

QUEEN VICTORIA (GOD BLESS HER!)

She was 4ft 10 or 11in and came up to Prince Albert's chest (when he let her!). She became queen at the age of 18 and by the time Lestrade was born (they never met) was a married woman with five children. The three main elements of her life were: wife to Albert; queen of England and later Empress of India; mother to her eventual toll of nine children. She carried out her duties in that order, loathed babies and toddlers and found it funny if people fell over or caught their fingers in doors. Rather than not being amused (one quote in thousands of diary entries) she liked her humour slapstick.

Victoria wasn't very bright. She was not a bad watercolourist, could play the piano and sing, like all well-brought-up gels of a certain class and spoke reasonable French and better German – her mother, husband and several courtiers were of the Hunnish persuasion. Her three great prime ministers worshipped her, but she didn't like Robert Peel at first and positively loathed Gladstone (qv). Only Disraeli (qv) got smiles from her because he flattered her nauseatingly and she fell for it. As the mother of princes and princesses who married into European royalty, she was linked by blood to just about anybody who was anybody by the time of her death.

She was also the Great White Mother – even the Sioux medicine man and chief Sitting Bull called her that – and her statues and portraits appeared everywhere from Alberta to New South Wales via parts of the old Empire now forgotten.

The great sadness of her life was the untimely death of Albert in 1861. Umpteen causes have been put forward here – she blamed her eldest son, Bertie – but she was utterly lost without the Prince Consort. She became, in Kipling's (qv) phrase, 'the widow at Windsor' refusing to take part in public life. Even Privy Council meetings were held, bizarrely, with the queen in another room from her councillors. She wore funereal black for the rest of her life, setting a trend which delighted the undertakers (see **The Victorian Way of Death**). So out of touch did she become that there were rumblings of Republicanism and/or demands for the Prince of Wales to step up to the royal plate and become Edward VII forty years before he actually did.

She weathered that storm only because she was brought out of 'retirement' by the smooth talking of Disraeli as her Prime Minister and the plain 'I call a spade a spade' speaking of Albert's Highland ghillie, John Brown. *Their* relationship spread rumours and behind her back she was known as Mrs Brown – hence the film of the same name.

As her reign continued and the Empire grew, Victoria became a symbol of greatness. Her jubilees were full of pomp, stuffed shirts, foreign nobs and miles of bunting. And the sun always shone on them – 'Queen's weather'. She died at her 'dear Osborne' in the Isle of Wight in January 1901 and the hearse taking her to the ferry broke down. A handy team of sailors replaced the horses and that is still the trend for royal funerals today. Until our present queen, God Bless Her, Victoria's was the longest reign in British history. Millions mourned her passing, but millions more – her own eldest son among them – probably said, 'Thank God! About time!'

Arthur of Connaught

I've always had rather a soft spot for Queen Victoria's (God Bless Her!) seventh child, if only because there is a photograph of him somewhere in full dress uniform having a crafty fag! He employs Lestrade to investigate dodgy goings-on in the Royal household north of the border in *The Gift of the Prince* and pops into the Coal Hole in the Strand in the full dress uniform of the Rifle Brigade, hoping not to draw attention to himself.

He was born in Buckingham Palace four years before Lestrade (who *wasn't* born in Buckingham Palace) and was, reportedly, his mother's favourite child. With a naturally military bent, he spent two years at 'the Shop', the Engineers' school at Woolwich and joined, aptly enough, the Royal Engineers in 1868. He served with various units in South Africa, Canada, Egypt and India. Created the Duke of Connaught and Strathearn in 1874, he was also Duke of Sussex and was later in line for the throne of Saxe-Coburg Gotha (Prince Albert's home). He married Princess Louise Margaret of Prussia and the couple had three children.

When big brother Bertie became king in 1901, Arthur took over as Masonic Grand Master of the United Lodge of England and he was re-elected in this role thirty-seven times by the time he was ninety.

'HEIGH HO FOR THE OPEN ROAD!'

One of the characteristics shared by Sholto Lestrade and Kenneth Graham's Toad from *The Wind in the Willows* is that neither of them can drive properly. To be fair, it's not entirely their fault. There were no compulsory driving tests until 1934 and not even a formal Highway Code until 1931, so there was a sometimes deadly free-for-all on the roads, kept within bounds by the relative rarity of the motor car.

The early pioneers of steam-propelled road travel were the Frenchman Nicholas Cugnot and the Englishman Richard Trevithick. Their work and that of other engineers was completely superseded by the 1870s by the invention of the internal combustion engine. Gottlieb Daimler's engine using vaporised petrol proved a success in 1884 and Carl Benz built his first two seater a year later. Not to be outdone, the Frenchmen Packard and Levassier went into production on their side of the Rhine and were belting out over a hundred cars a year by 1888.

A certain cachet developed from 1894 when the French set up motor racing between Paris and Rouen. A Packard won the following year, covering the 732 miles at an eye-popping fifteen miles an hour. Trains could go faster and so could horses over short distances, but it was the staying power of the car and the fact that it could travel from house to house, shop to shop and domicile to workplace that made it so practical and versatile.

In Britain, of course, we had the Red Flag Act of 1865 in which a man walked ahead of propelled road vehicles carrying a scarlet flag as a warning to pedestrians and other road users.* Edward Brother's motor tricycle of 1887 should have been a success, but its engine tried to do more than the 4mph speed limit so it never really caught on. 1896 saw the limit increased to a heady 14mph, much to the annoyance of the National Union of Red Flag and Other Medieval Obstruction Operatives of Great Britain, known for short as the NUORFAOMOOGB (not really!). That was the year that saw the first London to Brighton rally in November. Of forty entrants, only sixteen finished the course, the others dying of various causes by the roadside.

The Motor Car Act of 1903 increased the speed limit to 20mph and driving licences were now compulsory. 'Dangerous driving' was added to a long list of criminal behaviours that the police had to look out for. They set up speed traps, in the absence of CCTV technology, which even the Royal Automobile Club warned motorists about.

Lestrade drove a Lanchester, given to him by a grateful nation. He was never fully at home with it and although today's motorists would find the controls very simple, having to carry water and petrol (filling stations were rare indeed) and crank the engine with a handle to start the thing was

---

* This is the Victorian equivalent of the modern 'Twenty is Plenty' mentality. We are actually going backwards!

an inconvenience too far. The Lanchester didn't even have a steering wheel; just a rudder! Rich men like Harry Bandicoot drove far more impressive machines – Harry has a Rolls Royce Silver Ghost – and for those who did not care to drive, a uniformed chauffeur was de rigeur.

The Mirror of Murder

1906
Beyond the mountains of the moon...

'*Right*, gentlemen. Recapping by numbers.' Superintendent Lestrade, in martinet mood, was driving his minions.

'Murder One. Four victims, Captain Orange, late of the merchant service and his three nieces, when the harness of their trap broke on a downhill gradient near Peter Tavy, Devon.'

'Clues?'

'A tall man seen near the Captain's horse shortly before the trap left. He could have cut the harness.'

'And?'

'A broken mirror found in the Captain's breast pocket.'

'Murder Two, sir. Janet Calthrop, fell downstairs at King's College, London, on the way to the boudoir of her lover. Tripwire across the stairs. Broken neck.'

'Clues?'

'One broken mirror found in said lover's boudoir.'

'Murder Three. Juan Thomas de Jesus-Lopez, honorary major in the Sixteenth Lancers; body found in a ruined lighthouse near Beachy Head.'

The clues accumulate; so do the mirrors and the murders...
And the suspects.

'Mirror, mirror on the wall,' mused Sholto Lestrade. 'Who's the guiltiest of them all?'

He was to find out…

Inventions of the Devil

Throughout the Lestrade series, a number of dastardly devices have been employed to murder the unwary. They are all real and can be found in a variety of museums throughout the land.

1901
Hornby's Improved Toy or Educational Device for Children and Young People

Not actually a murder weapon, it is known today as Meccano – and just as well. Imaging putting the original name in a letter to Santa! Hornby's link to Lestrade is that he made a motorised Bath chair for the Superintendent after he broke his leg falling off the Titanic – **SPOILER ALERT** – *Lestrade and the Leviathan* and *Lestrade and the Brother of Death*.

More details may be had from: Frank Hornby, 10, Elmbank Rd, Sefton, Liverpool.

1904
Huish and Steven's Device for Preventing Self Abuse in Horses

Not a murder weapon, but gave a nasty electric shock to the disgusting, degenerate horse involved. I merely mention it here because Messrs Charles Huish, Surgical Instrument

Maker of 12, Red Lion Square and Frank Stevens, Electrical Engineer of 4, Princess Rd, Kilburn, often helped Lestrade with his enquiries.

1905
Bhisey's Improved Bust-Improver

Long before silicon, this handy little gizmo increased the flow of blood through the mammary glands. It contained a shield which was coated in glycerine to give an airtight join. Coat it with something poisonous of course and you have a murder method in *Lestrade and the Deadly Game*.

For more information, please contact William Sackville, 15, Girdler's Rd, W. Kensington, London, whose idea Bhisey pinched.

1905
Bhisey's New Instrument for Curing or Alleviating Headache

A clasping device that applied pressure to the temples. Used gently, it might have worked. Used carelessly (or by someone with murder in mind) it can leave a very nasty mess indeed, as in *Lestrade and the Mirror of Murder*. Any complaints should be addressed (not forgetting SAE) to: Shankar Abaji Bhisey, Engineer, of 323, Essex Rd, Islington.

Diabolo
Probably dating from twelfth century China, this was a harmless children's toy played with a length of twine attached to two wooden handles. The idea was to keep a wooden spool spinning on the stretched twine for as long as possible (see **How to Keep an Idiot Amused**). Substitute the steel spool for a wooden one however, and you have a rather vicious catapult, as in *Lestrade and the Leviathan*.

Ping Pong

Also known as Whiff-whaff and introduced around 1870, this game was all the rage, having bats that had vellum stretched over their frames rather like a drum skin. The skins broke frequently. No harm done, except for having to buy a new pair, but insert a deadly gas under pressure and the result could be lethal, as in *Lestrade and the Deadly Game.*

For replacement bats, contact Messrs Hamley, Toy Sellers of Regent Street, London. For cyanide gas, talk to your local, completely oblivious, pharmacist.

NB

The advertisers wish to point out that Brune's Device for Lifting Ladies' Skirts (1904) involved the use of three hinged bars *by the wearer herself* and not some passing pervert. For further clarification, see: Paul Brune, 19, Friesenplatz, Cöln, Germany.

JOHN BUCHAN

John Buchan, later Baron Tweedsmuir, was born in Perth (the real one, that is, in Scotland) in August 1875. He attended the University of Glasgow and Brasenose, Oxford, before becoming private secretary to Alfred Milner, High Commissioner for South Africa, in 1901. He was called to the Bar in that year, but never practised, continuing, with his wife and children, in various diplomatic posts, mostly in Canada, where he eventually became Governor-General.

His novels were very much of their time, the best known being *The Thirty Nine Steps* which covered the espionage of the pre-First World War era. It was his African adventure *Prester John*, written in 1910, that led to his meeting with Lestrade, however.

To reveal more would spoil the plot of *The Mirror of Murder*. My lips are sealed, along with those of Richard Hannay and Sandy Clanroyden.

The Deadly Game

1908
'The Games a-foot'
Sherlock Holmes, pinched from Shakespeare
(who probably pinched it from Kit Marlowe)

*T*he Papers call it suicide. The deceased's father doesn't. But when Inspector Lestrade of Scotland Yard investigates the death by duelling pistol of Anstruther Fitzgibbon, 27, son of the Marquess of Bolsover, his suspicions of foul play are immediately aroused.

One of Britain's leading athletes, 'nimbler than a wallaby on heat', Fitzgibbon is the first victim in a series of murders which threatens to extinguish the exhilaration of the Olympic Games held in London that glorious summer of 1908.

As the capital plays host to an army of athletes from the Empire, Europe and the United States, international politics rears its ugly head; a respected German journalist is discovered with an ornate paper-knife embedded in his back. When a hurdler of the Ladies' Team falls victim to her own bust improver (dubbed 'the killer corset') fingers are pointed in all directions and not least of Lestrade's worries is that his leading lady's husband is an American detective with a short temper and the physique of a brick privy.

THE OLYMPIC GAMES

The original games were, of course, Greek; a means to display the athletic prowess of warriors in the ancient world. To that end, the javelin and the discus were among the events that were featured in the first modern Games, held in 1896 in Athens. Twelve countries took part, although the Greeks themselves, ironically, won nothing in the medal tables. The Americans won nine golds, from nine sports.

A large number of athletes in the early years were gentlemen with university degrees. These men of relative inactivity were the only ones with the time to practise in their chosen field.

In 1900, Paris hosted the Games and an Englishwoman, Charlotte Cooper, won gold for lawn tennis. The athletes were hideously overdressed by modern (Lycra) standards, Ms Cooper wearing a smart, mutton-chop-sleeved blouse with stand collar, teamed with a full length skirt. The chaps had sleeveless vests but shorts reached to the knee. There were, after all, standards of propriety and it was accepted by many in the medical fraternity that revealing too much bare flesh was bad for one. Again, the Americans dominated, Alvin Kraenzlein (all-American!) becoming the first all-rounder with dazzling hurdling and long jump techniques.

1904 saw the Games held in St Louis and the Americans won the marathon. Actually, they cheated. Their gold medallist Thomas Hicks was born in Birmingham – the real one, that is. Rules were a little lax, to say the least. At least one runner had a lift in a car full of reporters and only ran the last section. He was disqualified for life (actually, until 1905).

The Games featured in *The Deadly Game* were held in London in 1908. The controversial 400 metres, won by Lieutenant Wyndham Halswell after some appallingly bad sportsmanship by the American contestant, forms part of the storyline. In the marathon, the 'plucky little Italian', Dorando Pietin (also part of the storyline) had to be helped to the tape by officials. He should, of course, have been disqualified, but Queen Alexandra (God Bless Her!) gave him a cup anyway.

Britain swept the board in sailing and while cricket, as a peculiarly English game, has never been included in the Olympics, cricketer J.W.H.T Douglas won gold at boxing. He was a very cautious batsman; wags said that his initials stood for 'Johnny Won't Hit Today'.

You can't win 'em all!

SCOUTING FOR BOYS

'He of the Big Hat' was Robert Baden-Powell, three years younger than Lestrade, a competent and much-decorated soldier who reached immortality by founding the Boy Scout movement. In our cynical, twisted age, when the only crime in town is historic child abuse, the exact meaning of his book title *Scouting for Boys* has been called into question.

Baden-Powell, serving with the 13th Hussars and later the 5th Dragoon Guards in India, saw more than his fair share of action and became the hero of Mafeking during the Boer War. Since scouting and reconnaissance were very much the duties of light cavalry, Baden-Powell took the lessons to heart and became fascinated with woodcraft. The boys of Britain were a particularly seedy lot in the early years of the twentieth century, especially in the towns and cities. Undernourished and poor, they made sorry recruits at the start of the First World War even *after* Baden-Powell's organization tried to make men of them.

Setting up camp at Brownsea Island in the summer of 1907, the hero of Mafeking set to work to improve the nation's youth. Three years later, his sister Agnes set up the Girl Guides, to remind everybody that this *was* the twentieth century and sexual equality was only nearly a century away.

Editor's note: some readers of *The Deadly Game* expressed surprise that the Chief Scout of the World (as he had become by 1920) wore ladies' dresses. It's true though, setting the tone perhaps for the LGBT trend of today. Some of us, of course, thought that LGBT was a sandwich.

Victorian and Edwardian CSI*

Today, thanks to endless Box Sets, we are all armchair forensic experts. Weirdly lit labs, from San Francisco to Miami (via London and occasionally Midsomer) are full of attractive people in white coats doing virtually impossible science in forty-five minutes. It is not quite like that in reality and it certainly wasn't in Lestrade's day.

There was no shortage of books on the topic. One of the most comprehensive was *Principles of Forensic Medicine* by Ferrier and Smith, written ten years before Lestrade was born. It covered everything from how to establish the identity of a corpse to complex chemical analysis in poison cases. There was a huge gap however between experts in narrow medico-legal fields and the average GP; an even further gap between the best-informed detective and the average copper on the beat. The merest glimpse of a police training film from the 1930s of how scenes of crime were dealt with has us howling in disbelief; at best, dozens of size eleven boots are destroying evidence before our very eyes.

---

* Crime Scene Ineptitude – a bit unkind to the police of Lestrade's day. They were *far* ahead of earlier generations.

There was no fingerprint technology before Sir Edward Henry (qv) introduced it to the Yard in 1892; not until 1905 would a guilty verdict be brought in on that evidence alone (the Stratton brothers for the murder of Thomas and Ann Farrow). Defective typewriter keys were the work of a fiction writer, Arthur Conan Doyle (qv) long before real policemen realised such observation could be useful.

One of the pioneers of crime scene investigation was Professor Rudolf Virchow of Berlin, who, as an archaeologist, had worked on the excavation of Hissarlik (Troy). Most of the police surgeons and some of the detectives working on the Ripper case used his techniques. To see Victorian CSI in action, let us look at one case that continues to baffle, not least because no *actual* crime scene could be found.

At the time and since, the media and the ghoulish public believed that the torso found under the arches at Pinchin Street in the East End on 10 September 1889 was the work of Jack the Ripper. To be fair to them, the police and medical experts at the time *never* believed this.

Constable 239H William Pennett was patrolling the area that Tuesday morning and, at five o'clock, it was not yet light. His bull's eye lantern shone on a headless female torso lying on its front under one of four arches that ran beneath the Tilbury and Southend Railway Company's line and led to the Whitechapel Vestry stone yard. The right arm was under the body, the left alongside the trunk and a torn, bloody chemise (petticoat) was wrapped around the neck and shoulder.

Two experienced detectives took charge – Inspectors Edmund Reid and Charles Pinhorn – and while one had the area searched and various vagrants picked up, the other stayed with the corpse. The first doctor on the scene was Percy Clark, assistant to George Bagster Phillips, who had presided at various inquests into the actual victims of

Jack the Ripper. The body was taken to the mortuary of St George's in the East, the shell of which still stands.

Rigor mortis had come and gone, indicating that death had occurred about twenty-four hours earlier. The woman was assumed, by the size of her breasts, to have been between twenty-five and forty years of age. She would have been 5ft 3½in tall and her internal organs were in good, healthy condition. She was not a virgin but had never borne a child or suckled one. Her hands showed no signs of hard manual work but a hardening on the skin of one finger might have been caused by regular writing.

She had died from loss of blood. All the dismemberment – of head and both legs – had been done post mortem, by someone with the skills of a butcher or slaughterman. A rope had been tied around the waist at some point and both elbows were discoloured from constant leaning on them.

Because of the regular police patrols in the area, it is unlikely that the corpse had been left for long in the archway and that was certainly not the murder site.

The Pinchin Street body was the last in a series of 'Thames Torso Murders' committed between 1874 and 1889 at various places in London. No-one was ever charged, let alone convicted, with the crimes and the forensic, scene of crime evidence, detailed though it was, yielded no conclusive results.

The case is typical of the Victorian police's problem. They could identify items at crime scenes, but had no idea of their provenance; were they associated with the crime or left there beforehand or afterwards? They could detect blood, but could not clearly tell whether it was human or animal – the first work on blood typing did not really get going until the turn of the century. Doctors could identify a huge range of poisons of all types, but since most of these were available without prescription at local pharmacists, that was usually of little help. Faced with a frustrating lack of knowledge, the police came, they saw, but they rarely conquered!

Bernard Spilsbury

The doyen of pathologists crossed Lestrade's path several times, from a spotty 14-year-old at Leamington College to a fully-grown practitioner at the Home Office. In those days, the pathologist was more important than the pathology. Science has taken over now, with DNA and even more impenetrable stuff blurring the boundaries. In Spilsbury's day, pathology was far more of an art and as a courtroom expert witness, he never failed to impress with his certainty. Anybody coming up against Spilsbury, whether as the accused or counsel, could expect a rough ride.

The Crippen case (Walter Dew's) (qv) in 1910 made him a household name, but at least one crime writer has doubted the great man's findings, asserting the body in the cellar at Hilldrop Crescent, supposed to be the murdered Mrs Crippen, was actually a man! By 1947, still working and broken hearted over the death of his son in the war, Spilsbury gassed himself a few days before Christmas.

Robert Churchill

The 'other Mr Churchill' was a little ferret of a man who owned a gunshop in London's Orange Street. An acknowledged firearms expert when gun crime was highly unusual in Britain, he was consulted by Scotland Yard several times after 1912. The science of ballistics was new at the time and Churchill was to it as Spilsbury was to pathology. Most of Churchill's really famous cases – the Green Bicycle murder, the shooting of Bertha Merrett and the killing of PC Gutteridge, took place after the Lestrade series finishes.

GILBERT KEITH CHESTERTON

GKC could have had Lestrade for breakfast. In fact, in certain photographs, it looks as if he has. 'The prince of paradox' was a poet, journalist, biographer, literary and art critic as well as being an orator and thoroughly nice chap. He was also, more germane to the Lestrade series, a crime writer – the creator of the Catholic priest sleuth, Father Brown.

He was born in Kensington when Lestrade was still with the City Force and, as a boy, became fascinated with the occult and played with Ouija boards (see **Was Anybody There?**). He worked for various publishers, using his artistic and literary talents to the full. Famously huge (6ft 4in and twenty stone), GK was asked, during the First World War, why he was not out at the Front. His reply? 'If you go round to the side, you will see that I am.'

Chesterton and his fellow poet Hilaire Belloc have been called the 'two cheeks of the same bum'; George Bernard Shaw (qv) called them 'Chesterbelloc'. GK's novel, *The Man Who Was Thursday* was Irish Republican leader Michael Collins' (qv) favourite book. Mahatma Gandhi was a fan too.

Wearing a vast wideawake hat, Donegal cape and carrying a swordstick, he was famously disorganised. According to legend, he once telegraphed his wife, Frances, 'Am in Market Harborough. Where ought I to be?' She adored him, so her answer was, 'Home.'

The Fourth Estate

In his long and exalted career, Sholto Lestrade tangled with the Gentlemen (and one or two Ladies) of the Press on a regular basis. The relationship between the police and news media has always been fraught and it was certainly so in the nineteenth century. Famously, whereas the City Force co-operated with Fleet Street over the Ripper case of 1888, the Met were ordered to say nothing. If they had, Jack might *just* have been caught.

Ever since the printer Wynkyn de Worde (a likely story!) set up his stationers' shop in Shoe Lane off Ludgate Hill in the sixteenth century, that part of London became associated with the written word. Shakespeare and Marlowe bought books at Amen Corner in the lee of St Paul's and it was only a stone's throw from there to Fleet Street itself.

News was sold by ballad singers and street-hawkers in those days and even in the decade of Lestrade's birth (1850s) men carried 'broadsides' through the streets with the latest breaking news. You could hire newspapers from these men and return them, for a small fee, when you'd finished reading. Until the 1720s, newspapers were periodicals, appearing weekly, monthly or quarterly. The *Daily Courant* was the first real daily, sold only in London from 1702 and its circulation was about 800. Until literacy increased, large numbers of people had the news read to them by those who could read. It was quickly realized that advertising linked to information sold papers and made money.

The demand became insatiable, in the provinces as well as the capital and ever larger printing presses, powered by steam and electricity, were bolted to the floors of offices to churn out the thousands of pages required. A new method of paper production was found (from wood pulp) in the 1860s, so the cost of newspapers fell and sales increased still further.

From the start, papers had their political slant, backing Tory or Whig which became Conservative or Liberal as the nineteenth century wore on and including the new Labour Party from the 1890s. Individual editors stuck their necks out sometimes to back a cause – see Ernest Parke in the Cleveland Street case. Others were highly influential – G.E. Buckle of *The Times* and George Sala of the *Telegraph* were celebrities in any gathering and *The Times* itself, unofficially called *The Thunderer*, could topple governments. Thousands of admirals, generals, politicians and churchmen, outraged by a particularly adverse direction in which society was going, wrote to *The Times* to have their voices heard.

Artwork, in the days before expensive photographic reproduction became affordable, was essential. The *Illustrated London News*, the satirical *Punch* and its sister magazine *Judy*, even the *Police Gazette* (not actually produced by or for the police) relied heavily on line drawings and engravings.

Newsboys carried bundles of papers from printing offices to retailers and from railway stations to shops. By the 1880s, they were riding bikes to do it, bawling out the name of their editions to passers-by. Scares sold well and nothing more so than "orrible murder – Read orl abaht it!'

Foreign news was handled by the organisation of Paul Julius Reuter and do-gooders like Charles Knight were producing educational material at a penny a pop in the form of *The Penny Magazine* and *The Penny Cyclopaedia*.

William Howard Russell of *The Times* became the first effective war correspondent, reporting from the Crimea in the 1850s. Although some of his work was censored, much of it got through to a blissfully unaware public who, within days, read of the heroism of the Light Brigade at Balaclava and the stoic work of Florence Nightingale at Scutari. Russell covered the American Civil War too, but since he backed the South, lost popularity. George Sala, more cannily, wrote for the Union.

In the 1890s, the New Journalism (see **William Stead**) established a pattern we still have today. Tabloids like *The Graphic* and *The Sun* vied with each other to produce ever more lurid stories. Sex could not be discussed openly, but anything else was fair game and editors ran the risk of libel suits daily. The profits – and the power – were enormous. Mr Harmsworth morphed into Viscount Northcliffe and created the empire of the *Daily Mail*. His office at Carmelite House was oak-panelled and oozed opulence, as did the Boardroom. Someone once said of Harmsworth that he 'sold news like soap and distributed mad views like stardust'.

The same could be said of any editor of any newspaper in the land.

The Leviathan

1910
'To our wives and sweethearts – may they never meet!'

'You're promising me a peaceful one, eh? This Year of Our Lord Nineteen Hundred and Ten? Let's hope you're right.'

Unfortunately, his men can't fulfil Superintendent Lestrade's wish. Nor can his daughter Emma, who moments later brings him news of a tragic boating accident involving members of her family. In fact, Lestrade's lot is definitely not a happy one. He has a number of vicious murders to solve, including that of a man hanged in a church bell-tower; of a potential cross-Channel swimmer and of his old sparring partner, Dr Watson. Anarchists threaten the peace of Europe and the whole of the Yard is looking for 'Peter the Painter'.

On top of all this, Lestrade is roped in to help with the plans for the coronation of George V. His daughter is in love; and Inspector Dew needs help with the disappearance of a certain Belle Crippen. And while Lestrade has his hands full, a violent London cabbie lies in wait for the Assistant Commissioner. A Mr Frederick Seddon is letting out the top flat of his house to elderly spinsters. And new bride Sarah Rose wanders forlornly around the National Gallery, waiting for George Joseph Smith.

Hearts of Oak – the Royal Navy

The Royal Navy has always prided itself on being the senior service – they even had a pack of cigarettes called that in the Good Old Days – claiming descent from the fleet raised by Alfred the Great to see off the Vikings. The Navy chose to ignore the thousands of years before Alfred when man fought in his natural habitat – the land. It should come as a surprise to no one, then, that the army is actually the senior service.

'The wooden walls' of England was how Nelson's navy was described and traditionally, the British navy was second to none in terms of seamanship and gunnery. Nelson's spectacular victories at Aboukir Bay, Copenhagen and Trafalgar not only established his legend for ever but kept Britain safe from invasion until the airborne threat from Adolf Hitler.

When Lestrade was a boy, the 'wooden walls' were becoming metal – the Ironclads of the 1860s, with huge engines substituting for sail, were the way ahead, although the Admiralty, under their Arch off Whitehall, were as resistant to change as the Horse Guards were to army reforms. In 1887, the Carnarvon Commission laid down that the Navy must be equivalent in size to any other two navies put together. Ships were expensive and the dockyards of the south, which had built ships for centuries, largely disappeared in favour of those further north, on the banks of the Clyde, the Mersey and the Tyne.

The battleships, of the Dreadnought class from 1906, were the pride of the fleets, scattered as they were all over the world to defend the Empire. Gunboat diplomacy was made possible by these sea monsters. When the Greeks burnt down Don Pacifico's house in Athens in 1850 and refused to reimburse him for it, Lord Palmerston, the Foreign Secretary, sent the fleet! Faced with the destruction of Piraeus, the Greeks fell over themselves to shower Don Pacifico with cash. The message was clear – don't mess with the British Navy.

The first destroyer was the *Havock*, built in 1893. She was capable of 26 knots, faster than anything then afloat. Submarines were to become the terrifying new face of twentieth century warfare – the D class of 1912 weighed 620 tons and, until the invention of sonar, could not be detected.

Jackie Fisher (qv) at the Admiralty and Winston Churchill (qv) as First Lord of the same worked in tandem to produce a fleet that was the envy of the world. Drawn up in line at Spithead each summer, with flags fluttering and bands playing on deck, it was a formidable sight.

The Navy, like the other armed forces and the civil government, had its Intelligence unit, collecting data on foreign navies and doing its best to keep ours secret. The NID (see **The Secret Service**) was probably the most efficient of them all; Lestrade tangled with them, too.

Jackie Fisher

When you are given the monicker John Arbuthnot, all you can do is call yourself 'Jackie'. The larger-than-life Admiral of the Fleet has always endeared himself because he looks so *scruffy* and appears to have been a stranger to a comb. He was 5ft 7in tall and dysentery and malaria gave his skin a permanently yellow hue which some attributed to his being born in Ceylon (Sri Lanka)

He was very religious and a hell of a dancer, insisting that officers under his command take up the hobby.* He was a good sailor and keen on reform but by the time he met Lestrade, he had become autocratic. 'Anyone who opposes me, I crush.' The Kaiser (qv) admired him – surprise! He shot up the ranks, from Midshipman to First Sea Lord, where he presided over the arrival of the greatest battleships afloat, the Dreadnoughts. He resigned in 1917 over Winston Churchill's (qv) inept handling of the Gallipoli campaign, though, to be fair, it was his own naval commanders who were unwilling to risk their ships in the Dardenelles waterway.

Did he really drink the rum called Old Fatality? Would I lie to you?

---

* He'd be a natural on Strictly today!

WILLIAM STEAD

The man who went down with the *Titanic* in 1912 was the best-known pioneering journalist of his day.

In Lestrade's time, Fleet Street was the home of the Dailies – Harmsworth's *Daily Mail* being the first in 1896 – and lesser journals operated in their various towns and cities. By the 1880s, the tabloids vied with each other to produce juicy, newspaper-selling articles to boost sales – it was called the New Journalism and Stead was part of it.

The son of a Geordie Congregational minister (see **Religion**) he was fluent in Latin as a child and well versed in the Scriptures. From 1870 he was writing articles and became editor of *The Northern Echo*, based in Darlington, the following year. At 22, he was the youngest editor in the country. Guided by his religious principles, he pushed for the repeal of the Contagious Diseases Act, which allowed the police to arrest 'loose' women suspected of passing VD to soldiers and was successful in 1886. He backed Gladstone (qv) over his attack on the Bulgarian Atrocities (1876) which helped secure the nearly Grand Old Man's landslide election victory in 1880.

That was the year in which Stead became editor of London's *Pall Mall Gazette* (forerunner of the *Evening Standard*) and he embarked on a series of journalistic crusades. The best known of these – and the one that would land him in trouble – was *The Maiden Tribute of Modern Babylon* in which he highlighted the prevalence of child prostitution by 'buying' 13 year old Eliza Armstrong from her mother for £5. The articles caused a sensation and led to the Criminal Law Amendment Act which fixed the age of consent for the first time. On a technicality, however – Stead had not got the *father's* permission to 'buy' the girl – he was found guilty and spent three months in Coldbath Fields Prison.

It was in the context of the international peace movement in the years before the First World War that he met Lestrade and he was on his way to speak at Carnegie Hall at the request of President Taft that he had his first – and last – meeting with an iceberg.

MATA HARI

In my experience as a crime writer, most *femmes* aren't nearly as *fatale* as they're *feted*. Such a one was Gertrude Zelle (or Margaret Gertrude Macleod – take your pick). She was born to a respectably boring family in Holland and married a naval captain who treated her badly. They lived in Java and she took up the local exotic dances, taking the stage name Mata Hari and, once free of her husband, making her famous in the nightclubs of Paris, Berlin and all points Bohemian.

She became the mistress of a variety of German officers long before 1914 and passed information to them gleaned from a similar variety of British admirers. The French Secret Service had a fat dossier on her and put in an undercover agent to lure her into a trap.

When she arrived in England, Mata/Margaret/Gertrude was interned by Basil Thompson (qv) head of Special Branch who used his height – and Mata's deliberately low chair – to intimidate the woman. She confessed she was a spy, for the French. Thompson let her go, to neutral Spain where she immediately contacted the German naval attaché.

Back in France, she was arrested, tried and found guilty of receiving money in exchange for information from German Intelligence. She died a dignified and heroic death in front of a firing squad.*

---

* The Europeans treat their spies, however despicable, with honour. In Britain we don't; we hang them as common criminals.

Murderers' Row

1910 was a gala year for real-life (or death) murder and the highest profile cases are catalogued in *Lestrade and the Leviathan*. Each case is, of course, far more complicated than I had room for in that book, so here, for the record, are the facts.

Dr Hawley Harvey Crippen

Perhaps because the name sounds so sinister, perhaps because of the drama of his capture by Walter Dew (qv) Crippen is regarded as an arch fiend worthy of his place in Madame Tussaud's Chamber of Horrors.* In fact, he only killed one victim – his wife; the body in question might not have been hers; and there were even those who said, if he was guilty, Mrs Crippen had it coming!

HH was a mild-mannered American pharmacist (some accounts say doctor or even dentist) who had the misfortune to be married to Kunigunde Mackinotzki, a shrill,

---

* Astonishingly, this excellent memorial to all things murderous and macabre has now been closed because of complaints from parents – who shouldn't have been taking their children there in the first place. In view of the continued existence of the far more ghoulish London Dungeon and endless replays of grisly crime dramas on TV, I find this pandering to 'sensibilities' extraordinary.

demanding harridan who performed (badly) on the Music Hall stage (See **The Halls**) under the name Belle Elmore. Crippen preferred his demure secretary, Ethel le Neve and this is hardly surprising. Given Society's abhorrence of divorce, runs the usual argument, the only way to get rid of Belle was to kill her. This, police and prosecution contended, was what Crippen did. He bought hyoscine poison over the counter (as you could in those innocent days) and gave it to his not-so-beloved on 1 February. He then partly dismembered her, burying the body in lime in order to destroy it, under the coal cellar floor of their house at Hilldrop Crescent.

Crippen told Belle's friends that she had gone to visit relatives in America and then he and Ethel, realising that the Yard were on the case, fled to Canada on board the SS *Montrose* as 'Mr and Master Robinson', the slim Ethel in boy's clothing as Crippen's son. A Marconigram alerted the ship's captain and Walter Dew (qv) overtook the *Montrose* in the faster *Laurentic* and arrested them both.

The jury at the Old Bailey found him guilty but Ethel walked. It was the case that made both Dew and Bernard Spilsbury (qv) famous though it was hardly brilliant detective work and it is quite possible that Spilsbury's forensics were unreliable.

Steinie Morrison aka Morris Stein

Steinie was a handsome burglar from Whitechapel who often did business with a fence called Leon Beron. The latter was found battered to death on Clapham Common on 1 January 1911, his face disfigured with cuts in the shape of the letter 'S'. Inspector Fred Wensley (qv) interviewed Morrison whose alibi defence was destroyed in court. It was suggested that Wensley had 'put the verbals' on Morrison – i.e. lied about the evidence he gave – which was a tired old defence ploy even in 1911.

There were rumblings about anti-Semitism and who but an idiot would carve his own initials on the cheeks of his victim? Even Wensley believed that Morrison was an accomplice, not the actual killer. For these reasons, Winston Churchill (qv), then Home Secretary, commuted the death sentence to life imprisonment.

Frederick Seddon

If a scintilla of doubt remains in the cases of Crippen and Morrison, there can be none in that of Frederick Henry Seddon. A slimy and repellent liar, he owned the house at 63, Tollington Park, London, where Eliza Barrow became his lodger in July 1910. By September, she was dead, her substantial assets (bonds and property) passed in a very dubious Will, to said Seddon.

A bewildered doctor – extraordinarily common in pre-First World War Britain – had diagnosed acute enteritis as the cause of death, missing the two grains of arsenic obtained from patent fly-papers that had actually done the deed.

A jury took just an hour to find Seddon guilty and even then, he expressed a hope that the judge, a fellow Freemason, would urge clemency. He didn't. John Ellis (qv) – who nearly hanged Lestrade – despatched Seddon at Pentonville in April 1912.

Marie Fahmy Bey

All right, this one did not take place in the murderous year 1910 but thirteen years later, at London's fashionable Savoy Hotel. The accused was French, thirty-two and the wife of a playboy Egyptian prince, Ali Kamel Fahmy Bey, two years her junior. The couple were not happy and had frequent, fairly public rows, culminating in one on 10 July 1923 when a hotel porter heard three shots and dashed to the Fahmys' suite to find the lady of the house throwing down a smoking gun.

The great advocate Edward Marshall Hall (qv) defended Mrs Fahmy and elicited that the deceased treated his wife appallingly, once dislocating her jaw. Though Robert Churchill (qv), the gun expert, explained that anyone, even a small female, could easily have fired the .32 Browning automatic which was the murder weapon, Marshall Hall's theatrics so impressed the jury – not a dry eye in the court – that they acquitted her.

The *Daily Mirror* newspaper, covering the juicy case, concluded that it was not proper for an 'Oriental' man to marry a Westerner.

George Joseph Smith

The killer with the bland name went by a number of aliases. In *Leviathan* he merely passes through the story on his way to execution by the ubiquitous John Ellis (qv) at Maidstone in August 1915. A Londoner from Bethnal Green, Smith was a natural conman who used several names and personae to defraud, cheat and, ultimately, murder. His trial, at the Old Bailey, covered the sensational case of the 'Brides in the Bath' murders and even a spirited defence by Marshall Hall (qv) could not get him off.

He was done for larceny and receiving under the name of George Baker. As Oliver Love he married Caroline Thornhill, got her to steal from her employers and jilted her, leaving her with a prison sentence. He fleeced widow Florence Wilson out of her life savings in Brighton and married Edith Pegler, travelling in secondhand goods before tying the knot with Sarah Freeman in Southampton – he was calling himself George Rose by this time. He helped himself to her £300 and abandoned her in London's National Gallery.

In Clifton, Bristol, he married Bessie Mundy (he was now Harry Williams) but couldn't get his hands on her £2,500 because it was tied up in trust. He accused her of giving him VD and went back to Edith Pegler. A chance reunion with Bessie on holiday in Weston-Super-Mare in March 1912 led to a rekindling of their romance and Smith was, as usual, desperate for money. He bought a tin bath for £2 (half a crown off after he haggled) and drowned Bessie in it on 13 July at their house in Herne Bay, Kent. Verdict? Death by misadventure.

Richer by £2,500 from Bessie's estate, Smith was back with Edith by September and bought seven houses in the area rather as you and I buy properties in Monopoly. He also opened several bank accounts under different names.

Alice Burnham drowned next. Smith, for once using his real name, swept her off her feet in Southsea in October 1913, insured her life for £500 and went off on honeymoon to Blackpool. Snag – the guest house he'd booked had no bath, so he moved to one across the road that had the necessary mod-con. Alice died there on 12 December after the landlady noticed water dripping through from the floor above.

Charles James, as Smith had now become, married Alice Reavil in Woolwich eight months later. He let her live but helped himself to £78 and all her furniture. The last Mrs Smith was Margaret Lofty, who became the wife of the man she knew as John Lloyd, appropriately at Bath, in December 1914. She met her Maker in rented rooms in Highgate two days after the wedding.

So many cons, so many aliases and three dead women, all by the same means – Smith grabbed their ankles and pulled, forcing their heads down under the waterline until they died. The Press and the families became suspicious and all three bodies were exhumed. Bernard Spilsbury (qv) went into forensic overdrive at the trial, using a hapless nurse to show how the murders were committed – the girl passed out and had to be revived! This was the trial at which Smith famously ranted, 'I am not a murderer, though I may be a bit peculiar.' Indicted with the murder of Bessie Mundy, Smith was found guilty after just twenty minutes.

Alfred Bowes

In what could be classed as the first known example of attempted murder as the result of road rage, Alfred Bowes tried to kill Commissioner Edward Henry (qv) at his Kensington home on 27 November 1912. Bowes was a London cab driver and in those days, all such drivers had to obtain a licence from the Metropolitan Police. His was turned down and he became fixated on the nonsense that Henry, as head man, was personally responsible.

When Henry answered the doorbell, Bowes fired point blank at him three times. Two shots went wide, the third hit Henry in the abdomen, miraculously missing all the vital organs. Henry's chauffeur wrestled Bowes to the ground and he was tried for attempted murder.

Honourably, Henry appeared at the trial pleading for clemency, pushing the idea that Bowes needed the cab licence to look after his dear old mum. Bowes got fifteen years and was released in 1922, Henry paying for his passage to Canada for a fresh start (ah, the caring policeman). They don't make coppers like that any more!

The Brother of Death

1913
'I cannot sing the old songs
I sang long years ago,
For heart and voice would fail me
And foolish tears would flow.'

Claribel

*R*ecovering from a broken leg after his ignominious fall from the Titanic, *Superintendent Lestrade goes to convalesce at the home of his betrothed, Fanny Berkley and her father Tom, the Chief Constable of Surrey.*

It should have been a relatively peaceful time, apart from Lestrade's lack of dexterity in steering his Bath chair, but an attempt on the life of his father-in-law (that kills the butler instead) makes him realise that a policeman is never really off duty. What is even more puzzling is the arrival of a letter which simply reads 'Four for the Gospel Makers' – and it isn't the first Lestrade's been sent.

So begins one of Sholto Lestrade's most mystifying cases; a case that encompasses not only the present, but the past. Lestrade walks down Memory Lane to the time when he was a young and very naïve constable. He looks back on episodes in his career that never came to a satisfactory conclusion and that hold other clues as to who the sender of the letters is – because whoever it is, it is a cold blooded killer.

Watching the Detectives

The police were unpopular for years after the Met was created by Robert Peel in 1829. Among certain groups, they have remained so ever since. The problem was even worse with the creation of Scotland Yard's Detective Branch in 1842. There was something sneaky and unBritish about a plainclothesman. The idea was associated with Eugene Vidocq and his Parisian thief takers of the Sûreté, who used disguise and broke the law themselves.

There were originally only eight detectives at the Yard, the most famous of whom was Jonathan Whicher and they scored successes against the *real* Napoleon of crime, James 'Jim the Penman' Saward, caught the murderous Mannings and solved the Great Bullion Robbery. By 1863, the Branch was headed by Inspector Frederick ('Dolly') Williamson, a no-nonsense copper who laid the foundations of detection. Peel's idea had been to create a 'preventative police', patrolling Plods whose very presence would deter wrong-doing. The detectives formed the other side of the coin – to catch culprits once the wrong had been done.

In 1869, the new Commissioner of the Met, Sir Edmund Henderson, appointed detectives in the Divisions. They were better paid than the uniformed men – always a bone of contention – and got a £5 annual allowance to buy their own clothes. Clearly, this led to sartorial skimping – Chief Inspector Walter Dew was known by the criminal fraternity as 'Old Serge' because he only had one suit. Detectives frequently used disguises which sound theatrical to us but obviously worked well enough. Chief Inspector John Littlechild wore a butcher's apron or a cabbie's overcoat. Inspector Maurice Moser was so slick at this that he could even fool villains in Paris, disguised as a limping brick-layer.

It all came crashing down in 1877 when a trio of plainclothesmen – John Meiklejohn, Nathaniel Druscovitch and William Palmer – succumbed to bribery in the Turf Club Fraud case and became the focus of the Trial of the Detectives. Into the breach stepped Howard Vincent (qv) who set up the Criminal Investigation Department the following year.

For ten years it was unclear who ran the CID – was it Vincent as Director of Criminal Intelligence? Or James Monro (qv), Assistant Commissioner (Crime)? Monro's resignation in 1888 settled the matter – the CID was thereafter under the Commissioner's control.

In 1883, with on-going problems from Fenian dynamitards, Vincent set up the Special Irish Branch (see **The Secret Services**), eventually run by Chief Inspector Patrick Quinn, one of Lestrade's *bêtes noires*.

As technology improved, the detectives were expected to keep pace. *Punch* still lampooned them, especially over their failure to catch Jack the Ripper in 1888, referring to them as 'the Defective Force' and even Queen Victoria (qv) insisted they be improved. The Yard's Fingerprint Bureau was set up in 1903 after the introduction of the idea by Edward Henry (qv). The Criminal Records Department developed from the Habitual Criminals Register and became the most advanced and detailed collection of such data in the world. Before computers changed record gathering for ever, there was nothing better than index files stored in shoe boxes! Lestrade relied on them implicitly.

Although originally forbidden to write their memoirs, a number of detectives went into print and became famous in a way which would be unthinkable today. Both Littlechild and Moser (see above) wrote rather self-serving books and Walter Dew (qv) produced his famous *I Caught Crippen* years after he actually did. Frederick Abberline (qv) is famous today because of the world's obsession with the Ripper case and various detectives rose to prominence because of the high profile careers of barristers like Edward Marshall Hall (qv) and pathologists like Bernard Spilsbury (qv).

Sir Melville Macnaghten

Educated at Eton (ah, the aristocratic policeman!) Macnaghten became a planter in Ceylon (Sri Lanka) and joined the Yard as Assistant Chief Constable CID in 1889. His boss, Robert Anderson (Assistant Commissioner) never liked him, but his underlings did. Fred Wensley (qv) called him 'a very great gentleman'. His memoirs included the famous 'Macnaghten Memoranda' on the Ripper case (eighteen months before his time in the Met) and his assertion, based on guesswork, that Jack killed only five women. Various Ripper-related papers which Macnaghten appears to have half-inched were returned anonymously to the Yard in 1987.

Sir Edward Henry

Born in Shadwell, East London, the son of a doctor, Henry attended University College, London (ah, the educated policeman!) and joined the Indian Civil Service where he carried out a number of duties. Here he became familiar with the new science of fingerprint identification and brought this vital knowledge to the Yard when he was appointed Assistant Commissioner (Crime) in 1901. Two years later, he was Commissioner and brought the Met kicking and screaming into the twentieth century. He improved morale and training and brought in a fourth Assistant Commissioner. The Fingerprint Bureau, the first full collection of dubious dabs in the world, came into being in July 1901. Henry also pioneered the use of internal telegraph and telephone communication linking police stations, despite the objections of diehards who complained they would have all sorts of people ringing them up! He presided over many of the famous murder cases of the Edwardian period and nearly became one himself when Alfred Bowes (qv) shot him in the stomach in November 1912.

James Monro

Educated in Edinburgh (ah, the Scottish policeman!) and Berlin, Monro, like Henry, also worked in the Indian Civil Service. He was appointed Assistant Commissioner (Crime) in 1884 and became Commissioner briefly in 1888 before political clashes with Charles Warren (qv) and Home Secretary Henry Matthews forced his resignation. His memoirs remained undiscovered until the 1980s and make it obvious that he was a quarrelsome Scot who threatened resignation at the drop of a police helmet. He backed the demand for increased pay, which made him a hero to the boys in blue but in many ways he was his own worst enemy. His superiors were probably glad to see him go in 1890.

Donald Swanson

One of many senior detectives with a centre parting and walrus moustache, Swanson was in overall charge of the Ripper case from 1 September to 6 October 1888. He reported directly to Robert Anderson, Assistant Commissioner (Crime). Today, he is best known for the 'Marginalia' he wrote in Anderson's book *The Lighter Side of My Official*

Life – though how the savage butchery of East End women can be seen as the lighter side of anybody's life is beyond me. The Marginalia is totally unhelpful in unmasking Jack because Swanson managed to confuse the oddball wanderer Aaron Kosminsky with the equally deranged Nathan Kaminsky, aka Aaron Davis Cohen (ah, the dyslexic policeman!).

Frederick Wensley

Wensley – 'Mr Vensel' as the Jews of the East End called him – was born in Taunton, Somerset and joined the Met in January 1888. Though a bobby in Whitechapel at the time of the Ripper murders (H Division) he took no part in the investigation and had to wait until 1895 before he realised his long-cherished ambition to be a detective. A popular, efficient and 'hands-on' copper (ah, the nice policeman), he led many high-profile cases before promotion to Chief Inspector in 1912. In the post-First World War world, Wensley became the 'Ace' in the newspaper reports of the day (his underlings called him 'The Elephant' because of his long nose) and, as one of the 'Big Four' he became Chief Constable. Superintendent Ted Greeno, a member of Wensley's Flying Squad (qv), believed Fred to be the greatest policeman of all time. Needless to say, he was a great friend of Lestrade's.

Frederick Abberline

A Dorsetman from Yeovil and originally apprenticed to a local clockmaker, it is not known why Abberline joined the Met in 1863. Carrying out his detective work against the Fenian 'dynamitards', catching dog thieves, arresting cross-dressers and investigating murder, Abberline was already an Inspector with A Division at the Yard by the time the Ripper struck. Since he had spent years in Whitechapel, he was the obvious choice to head up the investigation on the ground, reporting to Swanson (qv) and an increasingly panicky Home Office on a daily basis.

He became a private detective after his retirement, working for the European branch of the Pinkerton Agency. In the context of the Ripper, he seems to have remained convinced that the wife-poisoner George Chapman aka Severin Klosowski was the Whitechapel murderer (ah, the deluded policeman).

This is the place to offer a belated apology to the shade of Fred Abberline. I wrote a biography of him some years ago and know him to be an upright copper of considerable ability. In the Lestrade series however, he is one of our hero's *bêtes noires*, an unpleasant and hostile obstacle.

Sorry, Fred!

Walter Dew

If I am unkind to Abberline in the Lestrade series, I'm equally offhand with Dew – even though Lestrade and I are very fond of him. Dew's initiation into policing was his attendance at Mary Kelly's murder scene in Miller's Court on 9 November 1888. Inevitably, however, it was as the man who caught Crippen (qv) that Dew has reached immortality. Finding the remains of Mrs Crippen (*but* see **Victorian and Edwardian CSI: Bernard Spilsbury**) he was the first detective to use the telegraph (ah, the techno policeman) to track her killer down, arresting H.H. on board a steamship bound for Canada in 1910. Known as 'Old Serge' for the suit he habitually wore, Dew went into print in 1935 with *I Caught Crippen*, a first edition of which costs a fortune today.

Let's leave the last word on the detectives to *Punch* however, in those dark days of the Autumn of Terror in Whitechapel, 1888:-

A Detective's Diary à la Mode

Monday	Papers full of the latest tragedy. One of them suggested that the assassin was a man who wore a blue coat. Arrested three blue coat wearers on suspicion.
Tuesday	The blue coats proved innocent. Released. Evening journal threw out a hint that deed might have been perpetrated by a soldier. Found a small drummer boy drunk and incapable. Conveyed him to the Station-house.
Wednesday	Drummer-boy released. Letters of anonymous correspondent to daily journal declaring that the outrage could only have been committed by a sailor. Decoyed petty officer of Penny Steamboat on shore and suddenly arrested him.
Thursday	Petty officer allowed to go. Hint thrown out in the Correspondence column that the crime might be traceable to a lunatic. Noticed an old gentleman purchasing a copy of 'Maiwa's Revenge'*. Seized him.
Friday	Lunatic despatched to an asylum. Anonymous letter received, denouncing local clergyman as the criminal. Took the reverend gentleman into custody.
Saturday	Eminent ecclesiastic set at liberty with an apology. Ascertain in a periodical that it is thought just possible the Police may have committed the crime themselves. At the call of duty, finished the week by arresting myself!

Punch 22 September 1888

---

* A novel by Rider Haggard featuring Allan Quartermain.

Margaret Murray

They don't make people like Margaret Murray any more. Born in Calcutta, India in the early years of the Raj (she was two years older than Rudyard Kipling), she studied Egyptology at what is today University College, London, under the distinguished archaeologist Flinders Petrie. She was out in the Valley of the Kings, toiling under a hot sun, long before Howard Carter got there.

She marched with the Suffragettes and got a better deal for female academics at UCL, with a bigger common room than the men. She lectured widely, at Manchester, Edinburgh and Dublin and in the 1920s became fascinated by folklore and especially witchcraft. Her thesis – that all kings up to Richard III who died violent deaths did so as blood sacrifices for a universal witch-cult – gripped the academic world and brought her instant recognition in the Sunday tabloids.

There was a lot of opposition to her ideas, although, typically, most people waited until her death in 1963 to give vent to their feelings. Her book *My First Hundred Years* is fascinating.

THE HALLS

Convivial evenings of entertainment, involving music, smut and drink had long been popular up and down the country and with all social classes. These had been held in large open areas such as Vauxhall, Ranlegh and the Cremorne in London, where nookey of all types took place in the Chinese-lanterned shrubbery. Private supper clubs provided similar entertainment – the Cyder Cellars in Maiden Lane, the Coal Hole in the Strand.

Entertainers were hired for these bashes and some songs became standard legends: *Villikins and his Dinah* (ah, they don't write them like that any more); *The Ratcatcher's Daughter* and Sam Cowell's creepy *Sam Hall*, about the burgling chimney sweep. Most of this stuff was hardly family entertainment and was the rough equivalent of most stand-up 'comedians' today, appealing to the lowest common denominator.

Saloons grew up in London and most major cities to house the acts and provide alcohol and food for the punters. Many of them were places of assignation and prudes like Frederick Charrington, checking them out in the 1880s, found all kinds of furtive fumblings going on in the upstairs galleries. The Rookery in St Giles, the Lowther Rooms in Adelaide Street, the Three Tuns in Fetter Lane, all these and more became notorious as centres of vice.

The acts themselves varied enormously. There was always an orchestra which could belt out anything, singers (male and female), dancers, ventriloquists, jugglers, contortionists, yodellers and clowns. Drag was popular (see **Cleveland Street**) and the whole thing was presided over by an emcee, the 'idol of the Halls' who wore full evening dress, announced the acts and kept order with his gavel.

At the top of their game were the *lions comiques* who were the celebs of their day. They drank to excess and wore outrageous outfits, on and off stage. George Leybourne had his huge Dundrearies (waxed sidewhiskers), 'the great Vance' his tight trousers ('kicksies'), 'Little Tich' his huge boots. They sang about men-about-town like Burlington Bertie and Captain Jinks of the Horse Marines. 'Champagne Charlie' and 'Cliquot, Cliquot' were riotous drinking numbers that featured in the fierce rivalry between Leybourn and Vance. One was dead by forty-four; the other (in the wings of the Sun in Knightsbridge) at forty-nine. Vesta Tilley (Matilda Bell) first trod the boards in 1869 at the age of five and usually wore the get-up of a male 'toff'. She was so popular that men's fashions were designed with her in mind.

Winston Churchill (qv) described Harry Lauder as 'Scotland's greatest ever ambassador'. Today, his comic songs 'Roamin' in the Glaomin'' and 'A Wee Deoch-an-Doris' are cringeworthy, but they were hugely popular at the time. The son of an impoverished potter from Portobello, Edinburgh, he was, by 1911, the highest paid performer in the world and the first Scot to sell a million records. Quite soon, Scotsmen started wearing the kilt and swinging a cromach (walking stick) because of him.

Taking a leaf out of the book of the Folies Bergere and similar Parisian nightclubs, the 'naughty nineties' produced rows of girls prepared to dance the Can-Can, fling their frocks over their heads and belt out, with suitable nudges and winks at the audience, songs like 'Ta-Ra-Ra-Boom-De-Ay' (written by Richard Morton, arrangement Angelo Asher). Marie Lloyd started late, debuting in 1885 but she became the Vera Lynn of her day with hits like 'The Boy I Love Is Up in the Gallery'.

Many of the phrases of the Music Hall lasted years after the craze vanished – 'Pass the Mustard', 'Paddle Your Own Canoe', 'Following in Father's Footsteps', 'Stop Your Tickling, Jock', 'By Jingo' and 'It's naughty, but it's nice' – the last being pinched for a television ad in the 1980s.

Cleveland Street – 'The Love that Dare Not Speak its Name'

The Greeks had a word for it. The Romans tolerated it. The Elizabethans hanged people for it. Homosexuality, like everything else sexual, was a taboo subject for the Victorians. Even so, in the underworld, it went on and gentlemen rich enough found such pleasures abroad in countries where blind eyes were turned or it was a way of life. The anonymous author of *Walter – My Secret Life*, written in the 1890s, gets up to all kinds of unlikely shenanigans (a Victorian Irish euphemism) but he draws the line at 'unnatural practices'.

Not so Ernest Boulton and Frederick Park who were arrested in 1871 for cross-dressing. The charge was 'conspiracy and inciting persons to commit an unnatural offence'. In court, Boulton wore a cherry-coloured silk dress with white lace trim, wig and bracelets. Park was classier – his flaxen hair was curled and his low-necked, green satin number was edged with black. They got off – there was actually no law against wearing apparel designed for the opposite gender.

Henry Labouchere intended to do something about all this. He was appalled by an apparent rise of homosexuality, especially in the 'Maryannes' Mile' centred on Charing Cross and the arches of the Adelphi. Even as early as the 1880s, the term 'gay', previously used to denote heterosexual prostitutes, was being coined by homosexuals. Labouchere was an MP and his Criminal Law Amendment Act of 1885 created an atmosphere of secrecy that led to its being dubbed 'the blackmailers' charter'.

Determined to cash in on the 'bestial appetites' of some men, Charles Hammond set up a male brothel at 19, Cleveland Street (sadly now demolished) where a string of errand boys in their late teens routinely 'went to bed with gentlemen'. Many of these lads worked for the General Post Office (see **Going Postal**) and three of them in particular, Charles Swinscow, Harry Newlove and Charles Thickbroom, became infamous minor celebrities when the story hit the newspapers.

The luckless detective in charge of the case was Inspector Frederick Abberline (qv). The boys were easy prey, but it was their clients Abberline wanted, especially Lord Arthur Somerset, known as 'Podge', and Henry Fitzroy, Lord Euston.

In a long and tortuous story cut short, power prevailed. Abberline's case was effectively scuppered by those above him and 'Podge' was allowed to slip away to France. The only meaningful prosecution to take place was that of Ernest Parke (no relation to the cross-dresser), the crusading editor of the *North London Press* who ran stories on the topic and was convicted of libel.

The corridors of power were more extensive in Lestrade's day than we are used to and the media less intrusive. There must have been several prominent men who walked those corridors who breathed a sigh of relief when the Cleveland Street scandal died down.

The Fabulous Baker Boys

One of the most difficult questions to answer historically is how an island as small as Britain could run the biggest empire in the world (see **The Empire on Which the Sun Never Sets**). Part of the answer is families like the Bakers.

Samuel White Baker sounds like a rugged hero from the pages of popular Victorian novelists such as Rider Haggard or G.A. Henty. A physically big man, he was always larger than life, although one blot on his escutcheon (via brother Valentine) has made him less well known than his fellow explorers, Richard Burton and John Speke, who also, come to think of it, had blots on their escutcheons too.

His first adventure abroad was to run a coffee plantation in Ceylon (today's Sri Lanka) but, restless as ever, he got a reputation as a white hunter of formidable skill (not to mention as a writer on such matters) and ended up as mentor to Prince Duleep Singh, the fabulously wealthy Rajah of the Punjab, on a shooting expedition to Central Europe. Here, Sam bought a girl (as you do!) in a Turkish slave market and his darling 'Flooey' (Florence) accompanied him on various Sudanese adventures before becoming the second Mrs Baker.

Sam's aim, geographically, was to find the source of the Nile (an obsession shared by Burton, Speke, Livingstone and dozens of others) and he literally fought his way upriver through dangerous swamps, battling slavers, crocodiles and disease on the way. Flooey nearly died before the pair got home and they had to marry quickly to prevent a scandal in the stuffy Victorian society from which Sam hailed.

Brother Valentine did not fare so well. A Crimean veteran and dashing cavalryman, he was accused of molesting a girl in a railway carriage in 1876 (the incident is covered in *The Brother of Death*) and he was cashiered from the army as a result. The fact that Val's regiment, the 10th Hussars, was the pet outfit of Bertie (qv), the Prince of Wales, and that the pair were friends, outraged society even more. The incident is so out of character for Val Baker I seriously doubt that it happened as described by the prosecution. He ended his days as commander of Egyptian gendarmerie, living abroad under something of a cloud.

Soon after writing a biography of Samuel Baker, I met the current Baker family and gave a talk with them to the Royal Geographical Society in London in 2014. Like Sam, and no doubt Val, they are delightful company and a fascinating group of people.

Dressed to the Nines

Nothing sets a period of the past like its clothes. In Tudor England, the Sumptuary Laws dictated what each social class should wear and there were fines for failing to obey. By Lestrade's time, all that had gone, but cost itself dictated who wore what. Every gentleman had his favourite tailor, who knew whether he 'dressed' to the left or right and the best of these were clustered around Savile Row in London.

There was evening dress, the black and white penguin suits, complete with tails, worn, even in a domestic setting, by the upper echelons. In public, no gentleman would be seen dead without his silk top hat and there were special collapsible ones to wear at the theatre. Ladies wore sumptuous ball gowns, showing as much bare shoulder as was deemed acceptable and appropriate to their age. Silk, satin, lace, taffeta, feathers, even real flowers, festooned the society balls of the London Season.

A man about town would wear an overcoat, an Ulster or a Donegal, heavy, partly-waterproof tweed. Astrakhan collars became the rage after the army's involvement in Afghanistan, with the brand-new galoshes to protect shoes and boots. In the 1860s and '70s, young men called 'swells' vied with each other with sprigged waistcoats, tight check trousers ('kicksies') and pointed, brightly coloured boots.

Until that decade, ladies wore the crinoline, a cumbersome skirt fitted over a series of hoops. Learning to walk elegantly in one of these was essential – a sudden sit down would reveal a great deal to passers by. To keep skirt hems out of the mud, ladies carried chatelaines, metal dangly bits at their waists that included keys, combs, scissors and skirt lifters (See **Inventions of the Devil**). In the 1870s, the bustle arrived, throwing out the backside with a straight-fronted skirt. Needless to say, such fol-de-rols were expensive. An army officer, for instance, was expected to buy various outfits – full dress, undress (not as illegal as it sounds), mess dress, walking out dress and so on. It took Winston Churchill (qv) of the 4th Hussars, six years to pay his tailor's bills.

The Victorians rarely discussed underwear but they wore it all the same. They wore combinations ('long Johns'), woollen all-in-one vests and underpants which was a variant of the swimwear of the athletically inclined. Ladies wore bloomers (named after an American) which reached to the knee. Their narrow waists – fourteen inches was the aim! – were achieved by corsets laced at the back and made rigid with whalebone. The first brassiere (another middle-class euphemism) was not invented until 1914. The more straightforward Germans called it a *bustenhalter*.

The middle class aped their betters in dress as in everything else. A riffle through the pages of the Army and Navy Stores Catalogue of 1907 gives us an idea of what was involved. Drapery and Haberdashery could be found on the First Floor, which included foreign delights from India, Turkey, China and Japan. Most goods could be ordered by post, beginning the destruction of the High Street that is nearing completion today. Coats for ladies were called mantles or visites. Feather boas were trendy, as were duster coats, worn to the ground, for the new craze of motoring. Today's pinko-liberals would have been horrified by the fur department − sealskin, caracal, chinchilla, fox, marten, marmot and mink were all available to grace a lady's neck and shoulders. An 'attractive coat' in tweed, to be worn open or closed, cost five guineas (£5 5s). a scarf of Irish fox, with brush and paws, was £7 15s. To really cut a dash, a matching muff (hand warmer) at three guineas was a snip.

The best ladies' fashions claimed to be hot from Paris, made of nuns' veiling and Valenciennes lace. There were tea jackets, Japanese jackets and various gowns had trademarks − 'Aneta' had gaugings (?) and mercerised muslin; 'Phyllis' was a nifty cashmere piece, sensibly priced at £4 7s 6d. It was *nearly* the time of the emancipated woman, so special outfits were available for walking, golf, tennis, riding and cycling.

Gents − all the drawn models have centre partings and military moustaches − wore velvet smoking jackets and a bewildering array of separate collars, of varying starched stiffness, with impressive names like Windsor, Durham, Shakespeare and President. Ties were flash as well − the Garrick, the Westminster, the Bedford, the Winchester. Outdoors, the hearty gent, especially the dedicated Nimrod (hunter), wore a tweed Norfolk suit, with plus fours and a flat cap. For everyday wear, he put on an overcoat, a Chesterfield or a Victor. The bowler hat was de rigeur in winter; the straw boater complete with striped blazer in summer. Girls dressed like their mamas; boys like their papas, although by 1907 the sailor look was in because the royal children set the trend.

The poor, of course, never shopped at the Army and Navy Stores and had to make do with one set of clothes, darned and repaired and hand-me-downs from older relatives. Photographs of boys wearing their big sisters' frocks up to the age of eight or nine are not unusual. For the working class, there were working clothes. A fisherman wore oilskins and knitted jumpers. Shepherds and farm labourers wore smocks (each with its own distinctive county design). Even at this level, men wore three piece suits when they could, both for work and for leisure. Most towns had their rag fairs – the East End of London was the largest – where clothes could be endlessly recycled. The meticulous list of the clothing of Ripper victim Annie Chapman compiled by the Met in 1888 gives us a good awareness of the appearance of women of the streets in the 1880s. She had: a black skirt, two bodices, two petticoats, a pocket tied around the waist under the skirt, lace up boots, woollen stockings and a neckerchief. Annie, of course, slept rough in alleyways on many occasions, hence the *two* bodices and petticoats for warmth. She was what we would call today a bag lady, but thousands of women dressed like her.

Today we would be struck by the conventionality and the discomfort of Victorian clothes. A gentleman had a dozen-buttoned fly to wrestle with, his trousers were held up with springy braces. Tying a bow tie took forever – one's man came into his own at moments like these. Everybody sweated in the summer – although, to be fair, gentlemen perspired and ladies merely 'glowed'. Only horses actually sweated.

Keeping clothes clean was a nightmare because of the material (often wool) used. Traditionally Monday was washing day with scrubbing boards and brushes and the ever-present mangle put to good use.

Lestrade and the Devil's Own

1913
'From his brimstone bed at the break of day,
A-walking the Devil is gone,
To visit his snug little farm, the earth,
And see how his stock goes on.'
            Coleridge and Southey

'*S*holto Joseph Lestrade, I am arresting you on suspicion of the murder of Mrs Millicent Millichip on January 13th last in the City of Westminster.'

Lestrade had never been arrested before. Neither had he faced the drop. But when a woman died in his arms in the middle of a London pea-souper, the Fates were stacked against him. Millicent Millichip, as it turned out, was not the only victim in a series of murders where the only clue was the Devil's calling card. And the Devil struck in such diverse places as the croquet lawn of Castle Drogo, the theatre of war games on Hounslow Heath and the offices of Messrs Constable, publishers extraordinary, in Orange Street.

The condemned cell at Pentonville is a lonely place, even for a man with a loving family and powerful friends. But are they powerful enough?

Getting the Hang of It

The man who nearly hanged Lestrade (**SPOILER ALERT** – *Lestrade and the Devil's Own*) was John Ellis, but he was merely one in a long line of men who carried out the death penalty on behalf of Her Majesty's government.

The first of Victoria's hangmen was the notoriously incompetent William Calcraft. He was proud of his profession and hung out a shingle, complete with the royal coat of arms, that read 'J. Calcraft, Boot and Shoe Maker, Executioner to Her Majesty'. He bred rabbits and was a regular churchgoer. His work was very public – until 1868 executions took place in the open air outside gaols and the crowd turned up in their thousands to enjoy the show, as their forebears had done for generations. There was nothing remotely scientific about Calcraft and more often than not, his hapless victim was left dangling, slowly strangling to death in the noose while the hangman grabbed his legs, trying to finish him off. He hanged the Mannings on the roof of Horsemonger Lane gaol in 1849, an event witnessed by Charles Dickens and William Thackeray. By this time, Calcraft was usually drunk, the only way he could cope with the butchery he was carrying out. Even so, he did the job, sometimes alone, sometimes with an assistant, for forty-five years.

His replacement was William Marwood, who first bought science to bear by using the long drop. This resulted in the neck snapping at the third vertebra below the skull and death should have been instantaneous. Marwood, unlike Calcraft, received no salary but he made a tidy sum selling off portions of the rope used in a particular execution and the clothes of the deceased. Despite being quiet and reserved, he became a household name and the joke ran, 'If Pa killed Ma, who'd kill Pa? Marwood.' All his executions took place in prison grounds, away from the baying crowd who could now see nothing. A black flag was hoisted over the gaol to let people know that the job had been done. It was Marwood who devised the pit below the scaffold so that the long drop would work and he used a metal ring and leather collar to fit the noose around the victim's neck; speed was of the essence.

James Berry was a shoe salesman from Bradford, one of 1,400 applicants for the job of hangman when Marwood died. Unlike his almost illiterate predecessors, Berry wrote extensively on his trade, the quality of rope and so on. He used sacks of sand of the same weight as the victim and practised beforehand to avoid mistakes. Even so, sometimes things went wrong. In his first year as executioner, James 'Babbacombe' Lee stood on the platform at Exeter and Berry pulled the lever. Nothing happened. Lee was returned to his cell and Berry retested the trap. Lee was brought out again. And again, the drop failed to operate. Berry appears to have been more shaken by this than Lee, whose sentence was commuted to life (he was released in 1905). Later that year, Moses Shrimpton faced Berry at Worcester. The hangman had miscalculated, perhaps because of Shrimpton's age (he was in his seventies) and the noose wrenched the head from the body, blood spraying over the walls of the pit.

Despite these errors, Berry was usually highly proficient. He took a real interest in his victims, often met them on the eve of execution and read poetry or the Bible to them. After his resignation at the age of 39, Berry gave lectures on his craft, including a magic lantern slide show. His business card, printed in a floral design in black, green and gold, read 'James Berry, Executioner'.

James Billington came next, a former collier and part-time wrestler, who had also worked in the rag trade and ran his own hairdressing business in Farnworth, Lancashire. He habitually wore a black skull cap while 'seeing people off'. He detested journalists and sued newspapers who wrote stories about him. He hanged the deranged baby farmer Amelia Dyer in 1896. His son, Thomas, joined him in later executions.

John Ellis, he of *The Devil's Own* beams out of Edwardian photographs with a gentle smile, huge, de rigeur moustache and dimpled chin. He worked at a Lancashire textile mill before applying for the job of executioner. A friend said to him, 'You would never have the nerve to hang a man.' Ellis replied, 'I would – and did.' He worked with William Billington from 1901 and won a kind of immortality nine years later when he hanged Hawley Harvey Crippen (qv) for the murder of his wife. By this time, the Home Office supplied a hangman's ropes and the practice of selling the stuff at so much a length was over. Less than a year later, Ellis hanged Frederick Seddon (qv) in under twenty-five seconds, then a record.

After his meeting with Lestrade, Ellis went on to hang a number of high profile criminals, including the alleged spy Sir Roger Casement and the 'brides in the bath' murderer, George Joseph Smith (qv). Smith said at his trial, 'It's a disgrace to a Christian country, this is.' It would be fifty years before the government agreed with him.

'Nor Iron Bars a Cage ...'

Most crimes in Lestrade's time carried a prison sentence and the great, grim Victorian prisons in which men and women wasted their lives, are, with modifications, still with us. Glasgow has Barlinnie; Manchester has Strangeways; the West Country has Dartmoor; London has Wandsworth and the Scrubs.

The older prisons were often built in castles, as buildings strong enough to hold inmates against their wishes and the prisons of the early part of Victoria's reign had communal areas for living and sleeping, in which the sexes mingled freely and the children of the condemned joined them there. As transportation to the colonies (first America, then Australia) ended in the 1830s, more prisons were built to accommodate felons. Mill Hill in London and Pentonville became the new-style modern prisons, in which, around a central administration block, wings radiated out like the spokes of a wheel. At first it was possible to put one man in each cell and this had to do with two systems brought in in the 1840s.

Although the idea of rehabilitating offenders was always there, most of the great and good of Victorian society saw the gaols as places of punishment and correction. The separate system meant that men could not congregate with others, not even at mealtimes. The silent system meant that no conversation could take place. While hard-nosed gaolbirds took all this in their stride, others cracked under the strain. Visits by do-gooders and the efforts of the chaplain were usually a waste of time. To reinforce the idea of punishment – and to exhaust prisoners physically – the larger gaols had variants of the treadmill or the crank. The treadmill was a huge hamster-wheel and prisoners had to stand, pressing down the rungs with their feet to make the whole thing turn; fifteen minutes on, two minutes off. The crank was a box raised from the floor and filled with sand. The prisoner turned the crank handle which pushed a paddle against the sand. It sounds pretty easy, but I can assure anyone who hasn't tried it, it is absolutely exhausting and after half a dozen turns, you're on the floor!

Women got their own prison at Holloway, thanks to the pioneering efforts of reformers like Elizabeth Fry but it would be a long time before the 'comforts' associated with modern prison life became widely available. Riots occasionally occurred. In a famous one at Albany in the Isle of Wight, the female prisoners went on strike, stripping themselves naked and sitting in the rain in the muddy courtyard of the building. The governor eventually restored order by sending in male gaolers (only the married ones, of course!) to wrestle the women back to their cells.

Going Postal

The Royal Mail is so-called because James I used it to keep an eye on what the Scots were up to in his absence – generally, no good, by the way – because he was also James VI of Scotland.

Postboys on foot or ponies carried letters and packages all over the country for a modest fee, but by Lestrade's time, the whole process had been streamlined and was the envy of the world – today's Royal Mail plc please take note! Postmen worked long hours (often riding bicycles after 1880) and there were up to eight deliveries a day in most parts of the country. Stamps carrying the Queen's head (God Bless Her!) were of 1d and ½d denominations for letters and postcards respectively. Parcels were costed by weight. The advent of the railways speeded up the whole process so that, in theory as well as practice, a letter posted at dawn in London could be delivered to Manchester by mid-afternoon. We call this 'the good old days'. The first airmail service was provided in the year that Lestrade retired (1919). In the year before he was born, red pillar boxes with the Queen's initials began to appear everywhere.

One of the most impressive pieces of post delivery took place when General Sir Henry Wilson wrote a letter to himself, addressed merely to 'The Ugliest Man in the British Army'; and duly received it a few days later!

The Telegraph
For extra speed, Lestrade and his contemporaries used the electric telegraph. The creation of this system is littered with famous names like Volta, Wheatstone and Morse. In America, the speed of communication killed Russell, Majors and Waddell's Pony Express Service stone dead. By the 1870s, signals could be transmitted at thirty words a minute, depending on the skill of the machine's operator.

The Typewriter
Correctly, the gadget with a QWERTY (or otherwise) keyboard was called a typewriting machine. The woman who operated it was a typewriter. The term typist didn't come into use until 1885. The first commercial machines were available in 1874 but didn't catch on for another decade. Remington, Oliver and Underwood were the most common and they all relied on ribbons, ink and the ability to 'touch type' at speed. At a stroke, they provided a good, honest occupation for girls who had previously been maids or factory hands.

The Telephone
'Come here, Mr Watson, I need you' were said to be the first words ever spoken over the telephone wires, by Alexander Graham Bell to his assistant in 1876. There had been earlier attempts at various gadgets, the name itself meaning 'distant voice'. When set up commercially, all calls had to go through the operator (another new job for women) at the Exchange. Wires were pulled in all directions to link up the speakers who could be hundreds of miles away. Like all new systems, phones were unreliable and there was the inevitable suspicion of new technology. Scotland Yard resisted

for as long as possible and it was not until 1934 that the famous Whitehall 1212 number came into existence, three years before 999.

Incidentally, for all Dr Who fans out there, the first police telephone boxes appeared in Albany, New York, in 1877. In the UK, the start date was 1891 (Glasgow) but the Met didn't have them until 1928, when the first Dr Who, William Hartnell, was already twenty years old – nothing, of course, for a Time Lord!

The Root of All Evil

One of the most difficult ideas to grasp is the purchasing power of the pound. Historians today sometimes use the 'multiplier effect' to work out values at current rates, but this, at best, is merely a guide. Below is a list of the currency in use during Lestrade's lifetime. Coinage was based on L (Libra = a pound, 20 shillings); s (shilling = 12 pennies); d (a penny, originally the Roman denarius).

Sovereign – a gold coin little used by most people.

Guinea – a gold coin worth £1 and 1 shilling or 21 shillings. 'The Fancy' (sporting and betting gentlemen) usually used them.

Crown – a silver piece worth 5 shillings. Four crowns made up a pound.

Half a crown – a coin worth half the above – 2 shillings and 6 pence. Eight of them made up a pound.

Florin – two shillings; ten to the pound.

Shilling – originally a Saxon term. Called a 'bob' in nineteenth century slang, it was worth 12 pence. Twenty of them made up a pound.

Sixpence – half a shilling; known as a 'tanner'. The Dock Strike of 1889 was a dispute over pay – the 'Dockers' Tanner'.

Threepence – half of a sixpence. 80 to the pound.

Penny – a bronze coin; 240 to the pound. It was a very common entry fee for the cheapest entertainment, e.g. the Penny Gaffes or the Penny Dreadfuls.
Halfpenny – two to the penny; 480 to the pound.
Farthing – the lowest denomination, a quarter of a penny.

All the coins above carried the sovereign's head on the Reverse and various designs – Britannia, a ship, heraldic flowers, a wren – on the Obverse.

There was no £1 coin – that was paper money, as were £5, £10, £20, £50. They were all larger than today – a typical money note would be the size of an A4 sheet of paper. Then, as now, all currency was made by the Royal Mint (except the forged stuff that came Lestrade's way occasionally!).

THE MAGPIE

1920
'There *was* a Front;
But damn'd if we knew where!'

*E*ngland in 1920 is a land fit for heroes. So why is one of those heroes found dead in a dingy London hotel? And why does his war record show that he has been missing, presumed killed in action, for three years?

The deceased is none other than the fiancé of Inspector Lestrade's daughter and when her tears are dry, she sets out on a quest to find his murderer. And as always with Sholto Lestrade, one murder has a habit of leading to another; a second body turns up, linked to the first. How can a woman killed in an air raid in 1917, be found with a bullet through her head three years later?

When a succession of foreigners is murdered with the same tell-tale weapon, has World War Two started already? Can it be Hunnish practices? Or the Red Peril? Perhaps the Black and Tans?

A colourful web of intrigue unfolds as Lestrade and his daughter go undercover in the War Office, the Foreign Office, a film studio and at the Yard itself. When Lestrade's daughter is kidnapped, the writing is on the wall. And the writing says 'MI5'.

The First World War

The Great War as it was called* was one of those milestones in history – after it, nothing was quite the same again.

In a nutshell, a lunatic 19-year-old, Gavrilo Princip, assassinated the heir to the Austro-Hungarian Empire at Sarajevo in June 1914. The Austrian government, naturally outraged, blamed the Serbian government (not without justification) and threatened invasion. The Serbs were allies of the Russians who threatened the Austrians with war. The Germans were allies of the Austrians and they threatened the Russians with war. The French were allies of the Russians and they threatened the Germans with war. The British said, 'Now, hang on, chaps; surely we can talk about this...?'

We couldn't. It was 'war, war, not jaw, jaw'. If you are confused by the above, I'm not surprised. Think of it as a playground punch-up in which the puny underdog gets his big mate to help him and you have precisely the international alliance set up pre-1914. The result of course was not

---

* Careful, Gentle Reader. If you come across use of this term before 1914, it almost certainly refers to the Boer War 1899-1902.

a bloody nose and a few tears but the slaughter of millions and the end of Empires.

What happened in Britain was that we had no choice but to go to war in August 1914 because the Germans invaded Belgium to get into France and we had a military treaty with Belgium (the Treaty of London, before you ask, 1840). In a burst of patriotic fervour, young men flocked to the recruiting offices. War was fun, you got to see foreign places and it would all be over by Christmas. The only part of that nonsensical bonhomie that was true was that you *did* get to see foreign places, except you saw it over a sea of mud, shell craters and barbed wire, later through the yellow visor of your gas mask.

Once the reality of war hit home, with appalling casualties on the Western Front, the volunteering fell away and by 1916 conscription appeared for the first time in British history. Those who refused – the Conscientious Objectors – were imprisoned.

The police forces were stretched as never before, partly because a number of coppers had volunteered for the war effort and never came back. Crime rocketed as opportunists took advantage of the situation, but it was nowhere near as organised as it became in the Second World War.

The government became as totalitarian as the next dictator by setting up DORA (Defence of the Realm Act) adding dozens of 'crimes' to the statute book and making life even harder for the police. Riding a bike at night without lights was tantamount to selling secrets to the enemy and the courts were crammed with culprits.

With a million dead, Britain missed her lost generation. There were widows everywhere, broken-hearted sweethearts and men with broken bodies. War memorials sprang up in every village and town and everybody vowed that such a war must not be allowed to happen again. Women, who had done such stalwart work in munitions during the war, were given the vote; by 1928 universal suffrage, that was a mere pipedream to the early Victorians, was finally achieved. People were emancipated in a way thought impossible only twenty years before and the 'roaring' Twenties heralded a brave new world (see **The Roaring Twenties**).

The Secret Services

As the Nazis had worked out by 1940, the British Secret Services (by then known collectively as SIS) were run largely by public schoolboys and Oxbridge graduates who had never *quite* grown up.

Intelligence gathering was actually a deadly serious business, a vital adjunct to war and foreign policy that had been going on for centuries. Francis Walsingham, Elizabeth I's Spymaster, can lay reasonable claim to be the creator of the modern espionage network but by Lestrade's time, it had become considerably more complex. As usual, the more fragmented the Secret Services became, the more the tendency to in-fight and to tread on toes occurred in proportion.

The Special (Irish) Branch

This unit was set up in 1883 to counter Fenian terrorism in the era of the dynamitards who were busy planting bombs at various British sites. Its first boss was Adolphus 'Dolly' Williamson, but by 1903, Lestrade's bête noire Patrick Quinn ran the show, presumably on the grounds that an Irishman was best equipped to catch Irishmen.

MI5

The Secret Service Bureau was founded in 1909 to monitor what Germany was up to in the arms race before the First

World War. The Admiralty and the War Office collaborated on this, but they later devolved their own separate units. The boss of the army section was Vernon Kell (qv), whom Lestrade met in *The Magpie* and he worked in tandem, confusingly, with Basil Thompson (qv) of Special Branch. Although dodgy in terms of justice, the arrest of all twenty-two German spies in Britain at the start of war effectively crippled the German war effort. The Kaiser was very upset.

NID

The Naval Intelligence Division was created in 1912 from earlier departments. It worked out of 'Room 39' at the Admiralty and inevitably concentrated on naval matters, especially on the 'U boat menace' of the First World War. One of its later members, during the Second World War, was Ian Fleming, who went on to create the most famous fictional spy in the world, Commander James Bond.

MI6

Responsible for overseas, as opposed to domestic, espionage, MI6 was previously M11 (causing all kinds of chaos on Remington typewriting machines). Its most famous director, from 1916, was Captain Mansfield Smith-Cumming, who signed documents with the letter 'C'. This became the standard code for all subsequent directors.

These organisations, shadowy and unknown to the public in those days, had to adapt to changing political circumstances. In the nineteenth century, the Fenians and mid-European anarchists took some watching. By 1917 with the creation of a Soviet Russia, Communists were the enemy. Long after Lestrade's retirement, the Nazis came under the microscope.

The Big Screen

By the time the First World War began, there were 3,500 'picture palaces' in Britain. The earliest films, from 1895, starred up to three people and lasted for less than a minute. By 1915, DW Griffiths' American epic *Birth of a Nation* starred 3,000 actors and extras and 175 horses!

The new cinematograph craze led to a huge demand for subjects. 1914's trade directory, the *Bioscope*, devoted 520 pages to firms which worked in some capacity for the film industry. The Lumiere brothers in Paris, Thomas Edison in the States and William Friese-Green in London were the most famous names working on early 'motion pictures' as the Americans called them. Films were shown in theatres, especially as part of Music Hall entertainment and the first newsreel, in 1896, showed the Derby of that year as filmed by Robert Paul. Working flat out for twenty-four hours, he was able to show it to an astonished audience at the Alhambra Theatre the next night. It ran for a then unprecedented two and a half minutes.

Such was the impact of the early cinema that audiences ducked under their seats to avoid the spray from *Sea Waves at Dover*. Others screamed when a train appeared to be hurtling straight at them out of the screen. When Queen Victoria (God Bless Her!) saw film for the first time in 1897, she found the images wonderful, but a little hazy and the movements too jerky. All this was caused by the technical problem of sprockets and spools passing through unsophisticated machinery.

Fairgrounds set up Bioscopes where, with film at 4d a yard, they could entertain wide-eyed punters on wet days under canvas. Wonderlands, Palaces of Light, Chronograph Empires and Coliseums became the forerunners of the later, greater, purpose-built cinemas. The first of these (which would become Gaumont) was opened in London in 1904. Two years later, Londoners could watch American George Hale's *Tours and Scenes of the World*, sitting as though in a railway carriage rocked by attendants to give the illusion of movement. Ahead, on a screen, were the moving pictures of the scenery. Over a thousand 'passengers' a day were watching this by 1912.

Cinemas quickly became similar to the seedier Halls – places to cuddle and grope in dark corners. In fact, back-row behaviour 'at the pictures' was a standard entry for teenaged couples to adult life until very recent times.

By 1910, continuous performances had arrived – 'This is where I came in' became a stock phrase on the lips of cinema-goers – and the Britannia in Hoxton was the first to provide the service. Early cinema served tea in the afternoons (long before the ice-cream girl made an appearance) and it was very cheap, making it a working class entertainment. The cheapest seats cost 3d, but various deals and promotions often cut this to 1d. The best, still in the balcony as for theatres and Halls, might be as much as 1s. (see **The Root of All Evil**)

The films were silent, of course, until 1927. Written cards told the story if the mime show could not convey it and ladies at the piano played suitable accompanying music – soft and slow for the tender farewells, crashing chords for the cavalry charges and shoot outs. Comedy of the slapstick variety was popular. Custard pies, banana skins, falling downstairs, the hosepipe with a mind of its own, all these and more had audiences rolling in the aisles.

Almost anything was acceptable to early film makers and their audiences. The exception was sex – 'The photographing of lovemaking,' wrote one observer, 'is shocking... Only poetry has the right to venture behind that veil.'

MICHAEL COLLINS

Michael Collins was 'the big fella', a controversial Irishman who lived and died by the gun. To Irish independents, longing to break with Britain and achieve their long-cherished aim of Home Rule, he was virtually a saint, the man on the white horse. To the British establishment he was the Devil incarnate and the in-fighters on the Irish side tended to agree.

At the time that Lestrade met him, in 1920, he was already a much-wanted man. Secret Service (qv) reports called him, with considerable understatement, 'brainy'. The youngest of eight children, Collins' father was a member of the Irish Republican Brotherhood, itself a descendant of the independence-seeking Fenians that the Special Irish Branch (qv) at the Yard had been set up to defeat. Moving to London in 1906, he worked at a City stockbroking firm and read Law at King's College.

Involved in the Easter Rising in Dublin in 1916, Collins was sent to gaol in Wales. On his release, he joined the politician Arthur Griffith, founder of *Sinn Fein* (Ourselves Alone). In this capacity, he advocated the use of 'physical force' and became director of the Irish Volunteers. As leader of this band of patriots/outlaws, depending on your point of view, he wore a soldier's uniform with his revolver strapped to his leg like an American gunslinger. He had a formidable network of spies which kept him constantly one step ahead of the authorities.

As MP for South Cork, Collins was made Finance Minister in a nationalist government which was still illegal (1919) and became Director of Intelligence for the Irish Republican Brotherhood in the same year. This was war and Collins' assassination unit called The Squad was set up to kill British agents and informers. In the year of *The Magpie*, there was a £10,000 price on his head. He was shot dead in still mysterious circumstances on 22 August 1922.

GEORGE BERNARD SHAW

George Bernard Shaw was one of those annoying people who are so proud of themselves that they want to change the spellings and phonics of the English language. He backed eugenics even before the Nazis got hold of the idea, detested religion and opposed vaccination.

So far, so peculiar, but GBS was the kind of man who liked to be contentious as most of his plays amply prove. Naturally, as an Irishman, he backed Irish independence and denounced both sides in the First World War at a time when it was unpatriotic and downright Socialist (see **Politics**) to do so. On the other hand, long after he met Lestrade, he liked both Stalin and Mussolini, so that doesn't hold out much hope for his sanity.

From 1906 most of his hugely successful plays, *Androcles and the Lion* and *Pygmalion* among them, were written in a rotating shed in his garden at Ayot St Lawrence, Hertfordshire (Shaw's Corner).

One of my few claims to fame is that I once had my hair cut by GBS's barber. He made a terrible job of mine – and, judging from the photographs, of Bernard Shaw's as well.

VERNON KELL

If the first director of the Secret Service, Gordon Mansfield-Cumming, was known as 'C', MI5's top man, Vernon Kell, was called 'K'. You can't say spooks aren't original.

A military man, out of Sandhurst and the South Staffordshire Regiment, he spoke four languages fluently – well, a fifth if you count English and took on Chinese and Russian too. Until 1906, he worked at the war Office analysing German Intelligence. Working with 'C', Kell oversaw the separation of the Secret Service into MI5 and MI6. The First World war saw him heading up the India Sedition section but he also worked with Basil Thompson (qv) of Special Branch at the Yard.

Long after he met Lestrade, 'K' had been too long in the job (thirty years altogether). The first thing Winston Churchill did when he became Prime Minister in 1940 was to sack him.

BASIL THOMPSON

Educated at Eton and Oxford, Thompson spent a year farming in Iowa (as of course most British public schoolboys did in those days!). He was a civil servant in Fiji and Tonga and on his return became governor of a variety of prisons. In 1913, he was appointed head of the CID at the Yard and worked with the infant Intelligence Service to carry out arrests, especially during the First World War. He interrogated Mata Hari (qv) and wrote a book he would never get away with today called *Queer People*. He didn't like Irishmen or Jews and became Director of Intelligence before Lloyd George kicked him out.

One doesn't like to dwell on a chap's little idiosyncracies, but in 1925 he was caught *in flagrante*, so to speak, with Miss Thelma de Lava (who was clearly no better than she should be) and was fined £5. Attempts to bribe bobbies didn't help his case; neither did the old chestnut about investigating London vice for a book he was writing. Oh dear and oh dear!

Lestrade and the Kiss of Horus

1922
'Look on my works, ye mighty, and despair!'
Shelley

'*And* death shall come on soft wings to him that touches the tomb of the Pharaoh...'

The wings that retired Chief Superintendent Lestrade came on were those of a de Havilland Hercules, named Olivia. The archaeologist, Howard Carter, had made the discovery of the century in the Valley of the Kings, but all around him, men were dying: Lord Carnarvon, careless with his razor, fell prey to a mosquito bite; Alain le Clerk left the tomb in a hurry to die alone in the desert; Aaron G. String, the railway magnate, blew his brains out yards from the tomb's entrance.

And so it was that Sholto Lestrade flew East to solve a riddle every bit as impenetrable as that of the sphinx. People remarked on the funny old Gizeh, in his bowler and Donegal, battling the elements against sand, revolting Egyptians and the Curse of the Pharaohs...

But could he avoid the Kiss of Horus?

The Testimony of the Spade

Lestrade came across archaeologists surprisingly frequently in the course of his career, most notably, of course, in the Valley of the Kings in Egypt. The science was more of an art in those days (like forensics, which it closely resembles) and was carried out almost entirely by men in plus fours and three piece suits. In hot climates, of course, linen tunics, topees and cholera belts were de rigeur.

Most finds were made by accident during farming or the cutting of a canal or railway line. None of the modern techniques, like the decidedly dodgy and disappointing geophysics, was available. It was all down to mattocks, spades and, for the delicate work, trowels and brushes.

Wookey Hole (*The Guardian Angel*)
Workmen digging a canal in 1857 found prehistoric bones – of mammoth, hyenas and man. In 1912, Herbert Balch found a complete female skeleton and household objects from the Iron Age. He had been working at the Cave since 1904, excavating areas known today as Hell's Ladder and Witch's Kitchen. A variety of Roman coins, from Vespasian to Valentinian II came to light. Arthur Bulleid, who features in the *Guardian Angel*, was a Glastonbury resident who worked on the ancient lake village in the area.

Welwyn (*The Magpie*)

The area that was to become Welwyn Garden City in the 1920s was rich in archaeology. It was near the Viking frontier of the Danelaw but had Roman and Belgic settlements all over the place before that. The particular site referred to in *The Magpie* was an Iron Age homestead on the slopes above the River Lea where Stanborough School now stands.

The Valley of the Kings (*The Kiss of Horus*)

Where do you start on this one? Howard Carter's discovery, on 5 November 1922, put all previous archaeological finds in the shade. The treasures of the tomb are invaluable, both in their gold content and in the information they provide on the boy king Tutankhamen and the way of death in ancient Egypt. Most of the tombs in the Valley of the Kings were robbed in antiquity, which doesn't say much about Egyptians' veneration for their pharaohs or their dead, but Tut's somehow escaped.

From 1907, the fifth earl of Carnarvon funded Howard Carter to dig in the Valley and sixteen years later, when money and patience had almost run out, Carter struck literal gold. Thirty-two centuries after his death, the world could gaze again at the gilded face of the king who died, according to some, in suspicious circumstances. Beds, chariots, statues, garlands of flowers and of course, the embalmed body itself, all appeared in the light of Carter's torches.

Immediately, rumours of a pharaoh's curse circulated and, in reality, people died in relatively alarming numbers, among them Lord Carnarvon himself. Spooky, or what?

FLIGHTS OF FANCY

Most people in Lestrade's day had never travelled by plane. In fact, until he was a Chief Inspector, most people had never even seen one. There was something alarmingly wrong with the phrase 'heavier-than-air flying machine' and those who flew them were magnificent indeed.

Everything changed at Kitty Hawk beach, North Carolina, in 1903 when brothers Orville and Wilbur Wright kept their home-made machine airborne for 13 seconds. It was feeble by modern standards, but it was the start of another transport revolution (see **The Underground**) and beat the hell out of jumping off the Eiffel Tower wearing a pair of Leonardo da Vinci-inspired leather wings.

No sooner had man learned to fly than he started to kill his fellow fliers. The First World War produced aerial reconnaissance for the first time* and brightly-painted Nieuports and Fokkers of various Jasta attached to the German army, took on the Pups and Camels of the Royal Flying Corps (later the RAF). Emma Lestrade's fiancé, Paul Dacres, was flying such a plane when he disappeared somewhere over France in 1917 (see *The Magpie*).

---

* Apart from balloons, which had been used by the military since Napoleon's time and to which Lestrade was naturally averse (see *The Guardian Angel*).

Military aircraft, in the form of fighters and bombers, went their own way, but Lestrade's other aerial exploits (apart from the balloon) took place on his flight to Egypt in 1922 in *The Kiss of Horus*. He was probably too old to fly by then, but, if truth be told, there was never a good age for it. The first commercial flight travelled between Hendon and Windsor (22 miles) on 9 September 1911, delivering the mail. Everyone thought this was a joke and the service was discontinued.

The Scandinavian countries were the first to provide a continuous service from 1918 and the RAF regularly flew civilians between London and Paris. In August 1919, Air Transport began a timetabled service between Hounslow and Le Bourget which took 2¼ hours. There was one passenger, letters, grouse (freshly shot on Scottish moors on the Glorious Twelfth) and several pots of clotted Devonshire cream.

By the end of 1922, airlines were operating from London to a variety of world stops – Brussels, Cologne and Amsterdam within Europe and (via various jumps) Cairo (aha!), Jerusalem and Baghdad. Since all these exotic places were effectively in British hands, it made more sense than it does today.

Early aircraft, like the de Haviland on which Lestrade flew, carried half a dozen passengers sitting in wicker chairs. There was a steward to serve cocktails and a siffleuse, who whistled various tunes, as in-flight entertainment (and to disguise the fact that the de Haviland was heavier than air, was defying the laws of gravity and was several thousand feet up, moving at a hundred miles an hour).

Worried?

Not Lestrade!

The Roaring Twenties

Lestrade was 66 (two thirds of the Age of the Beast) when the 'Twenties began, so he was unlikely to be a Bright Young Thing, still less a Flapper.

The First World War had changed everything. There was a Lost Generation of young men, women were on the way to emancipation and universal suffrage had at last arrived. Wealthier people could afford a gramophone, courtesy of His Master's Voice, even if they weren't quite ready for the cacophony of the Jazz Age. Ladies' hair was bobbed and Lux soap cost 4d. Retired colonels – and not just from Tunbridge Wells – reacted with horror at the scantily-clad lovelies at Hampton Court's Gala Day.

Noel Coward had arrived and London theatregoers had the joys of *No, No, Nanette* at the Palace Theatre to look forward to. The Socialist Douglas Goldring wrote that the 'Twenties were full of 'educationalists, Morris-dancers, vegetarians, teetotallers, professors of economics, drug-takers, boozers...gossip columnists, playwrights, Communists, Roman Catholic converts, painters and poets'. In other words, the world that Lestrade had known all his life was already going to Hell in a police handcart.

For the young and double-jointed, there was the Charleston and the Black Bottom and dancing became almost a national obsession. Nightclubs proliferated in the larger cities, causing additional headaches for the police. The actress Elsa Lanchester had one, the Cave of Harmony, in Seven Dials, once again a centre of thieves and lowlife. The Fifty-Fifty in Wardour Street provided cocktails, music and companionship for the luvvies of stage and screen. Jack Buchanan could be found there; so could Ivor Novello, Ernest Thesiger, Seymour Hicks and Gladys Cooper. Down the road, Ambrose and his orchestra played sweet music under soft lights.

Society photographer Cecil Beaton was snapping Anyone who was Anyone and Marie Stopes outraged everyone with her avant-garde advice on birth control.

It was the age of the car and the plane (see **Wings of the Pharaoh**). Harry Bandicoot's Silver Ghost held its own as a prestigious monster from a bygone age, but Lestrade's Lanchester was hopelessly out of date. Harley-Davidson were making sidecars for the aspiring young couple and Matinee Idol Owen Nares was fined £1 for driving his car at a shocking twenty-nine miles an hour. The Austin Seven and the Morris Minor were the cars of the future, cheaper than the much-trumpeted Model T of Henry Ford. The airship was the civilian counterpart of the Zeppelin of the First World War and before it was realised how desperately unsafe it was, commanded awe from little boys on the ground.

Ladies' fashions became hideous. Cloche hats and turbans hid the bob and long, straight frocks and coats were designed for long, straight bodies. If you didn't have one of those, hard luck. They had names like 'Mikado', 'Caprice' and 'Infidelle' and cost a fortune. For the chaps, a double-breasted dinner jacket without tails, called a 'Tuxedo' was all the rage. On their feet, they wore highly-polished two-tone 'co-respondent' shoes.

The political giants of the 'Twenties were still the men Lestrade had known years earlier. David Lloyd George, mired in the honours selling scandal, was a grand old man. Winston Churchill who had made a hash of the Gallipoli campaign in 1915 was in the wilderness. There was a Labour government for the first time, led by the Scots crofter's son Ramsay MacDonald and anxious whispers about a lurch to the left in tune with Comrade Lenin's new Soviet Union in Russia. In Europe, the League of Nations promised arbitration not war, the ballot not the bullet and America, having lent a Division to the First World War, retreated into less than splendid isolationism again.

Art Deco, all straight lines and brave new world, replaced the sensuous Art Nouveau of the 1890s and beyond. Buildings became taller, squarer, both pinched from the American skyscraper idea and prefiguring the monstrosities of Nazi Germany.

The Empire was vanishing fast, like the American prairie. Commonwealth, Dominion States, Mandated Territories – these were the buzzwords of the 'Twenties as Britain tried to accept that she was no longer 'top nation' and to find another role in the world. As if in defiance of all this, a British Empire Exhibition was staged at Wembley, opening on St George's Day 1924. Special cigarette cards were made to commemorate it. Every little boy pestered his dad and his big brother for cigarette cards, the obsession of the decade's youth. W.W. Wakefield of Harlequins Rugby Club was in great demand; so was J. Dimmock of Spurs. H. Sutcliffe batted for Yorkshire and A.P.F. Chapman for Kent. The ladies weren't forgotten either – Betty Nuthall and Mrs Mallory were high on the collectors' lists for Lawn Tennis.

In sporting terms, though, every boy's hero (and most men's) were Jack Hobbs and Don Bradman – and in those days, Gentle Reader, cricketers still wore whites, not the body armour of today.

Murder of course still went on, whether Lestrade was there to arrest people or not. Frederick Bywaters killed Percy Thompson so that he could pinch his wife, Edith, and they hanged him for it. They hanged Major Herbert Armstrong too, who was a little too free with poison in his home town of Hay-on-Wye. And Sunday School teacher Norman Thorne butchered Elsie Cameron. The Riddle of Birdhurst Rise and the shooting of PC Gutteridge hogged the headlines and police forces around the country kept the hangman busy.

A new generation of literati appeared, with variously important things to say about something or other. James Joyce flew the flag for Ireland; D.H. Lawrence wrote meaningful stories about the working class and opened the door to the milkman in the nude. Aldous Huxley's *Antic Hay* featured lesbianism, devil-worship and nymphomania, all three topics kept under *very* close wraps in the Victorian/Edwardian era. The Bloomsbury set were dominated by the Woolfs and Lytton Strachey (whom Lestrade nearly met) wandered around like a gaunt ghost from the past.

Britain's newspapers, no longer content to pass on news funded by advertising, vied with each other to boost sales. The *Mail* charged a crippling £1,200 to place an ad on its front page, but it had Teddy Tail for the kids and it would be years before he was upstaged by the *Express*'s Rupert Bear. The *Daily Herald* wrote for the political Left, publishing articles by the angry young men of the Lost Generation, like the war poet Siegfried Sassoon.

Cats' whiskers and battery-operated 'wireless' sets were the must have gadgets of the day, replacing for ever the wind-up gramophone. You could listen to the Big Band sound of orchestras like Henry Hall's and feel safe in the knowledge that BBC announcers were wearing dinner jackets as they spoke to you. So bad – and intermittent – was the reception, that perhaps only one word in five was audible.

Art went from bad to worse, prompting the Nazis to ban much of it in the next decade. Cubism was in. Picasso, who could actually draw, chose not to. Lowry gave it his best shot with his stick people. Dadaism came from Switzerland. And don't get me started on Clarice Cliffe!

The very poor didn't go anywhere. Neither did they enjoy most of the things mentioned above. The averagely poor went on charabanc days out to the seaside, to put hankies on their heads and roll up their trouser legs. Adventurous types wore back-packs (the bane of civilization) and went 'hiking' (a 'Twenties word). Travel agencies sprang up everywhere, offering tours of the Holy Land – much of which was still British – for only 49 guineas. Captain George Mallory disappeared somewhere in the Himalayas – his desiccated body was found in 1999.

Among the richer, younger trendier types, a whole new vocabulary developed. 'Goodbye' became 'Toodle-oo' or 'Toodle-pip'; things were 'ripping', 'topping' and a casual acquaintance was an 'old sport'. A party was a 'do'. The middle aged were 'elderly fruit'. 'Coo-ee' was the shrill cry of a friend from one side of the street to another, a sound, I must add here, perfected by my good lady wife; she has something in the timbre of her 'coo-ee' that makes all men freeze guiltily at 1,000 paces.

With hindsight, the 'Twenties *did* roar, as a means of escapism after the grim years of the First World War. It would all end in tears, of course, with the Wall Street Crash, the subsequent Slump and the rise of Nazi Germany.

LESTRADE AND THE GIANT RAT OF SUMATRA

1935
'So, Sholto, let me and you be wipers
Of scores out with all men, especially pipers!'
The *original* version of *The Piped Piper
of Hamelin* by Robert Browning

*E*verybody, they say, has a book in them. Retired Chief Inspector Walter Dew certainly did. And it took him back to the good old days, when coppers lived in station houses, that nice Mr Campbell-Bannerman was at Number Ten and Britain had the biggest empire in the world. But, under the streets of London, something stirred. More than that, there was a muttering that grew to a grumbling and the grumbling grew to a mighty rumbling. Then out of the houses, the bodies came tumbling!

Superintendent Sholto Lestrade, with Dew by his side and the rookies Bang and Olufsen in his wake, must go Below to face their demons, to find a murderer whose machinations will upset the infrastructure of the richest city on earth.

Will any of them live to tell Dew's tale? The tale of a rat.

Under London

Life below the streets of London features in two of the Lestrade stories, *The Dead Man's Hand* and *The Giant Rat of Sumatra*. It is one of the oddities of life that, while thousands ride on the Underground every day, very few know the extent of the rabbit-warren kingdom all around them.

The Thames has a number of tributaries which feed into it under London's streets. The Efra has a road named after it in Brixton but the river itself has long been submerged. The Fleet, an open sewer until the early nineteenth century, is now only known as the ex-newspaper capital of Britain in the street above. The Ty Burn, which ran past the notorious execution ground of the triple tree (marked today by Marble Arch) still trickles through Gray's Antique Market in New Bond Street. This tangle of waterways has been built over for so long that their existence is doubted by some – *but they are still there.*

Building and maintaining the vast network of water pipes and sewage ducts under the capital was a lifelong work. In 1902, it was estimated that every Londoner consumed in various ways, an astonishing forty gallons of water a day. Pumping and filter stations, ornate and huge, still litter the London landscape, usually because they are listed buildings, even if they are no longer in use. When Lestrade was a young copper, the turncock's job was to switch private water supplies on and off. Inspections of water pipes were made after dark by men with lanterns to minimise disturbance to residents (oh, heady, civilised days!). Water troughs were essential for London's squadrons of cab and dray horses and fountains were a lifeline in the appallingly hot summer streets.

Technology created ever more subterranean caverns. Gas, electricity and the telephone network required cables, tunnels and armies of workmen to install it all. The main tunnels were surprisingly airy. Men could walk upright and often travelled miles during a working day, parallel to the streets above. To aid navigation, they even used the street names – Shoe Lane, Leadenhall and so on. Other place names stayed when the surface version had disappeared, rather as today's 'ghost stations' on the Underground are still there but unused.

So complex is the tunnel maze that in some places, 'two-decker' London became three or four decker. Archways were made of brick, often tiled to reflect the lantern lights and the miracle of this is that, despite their age, most of them are still functioning.

Various writers of the time were quick to point out that working as a sewerman for eight hours a day was not the appalling job it might appear. Tell it to the Marines! A sewerman was as recognizable to Londoners as a 'hi-viz' road worker is today. He wore a shovel hat, blue smock and huge waterproof waders, carrying a torch of some kind and a stick, both to test pipes and to beat off the armies of rats who watched his every move. You could also smell him streets away.

There were various attempts to create pedestrian tunnels under the Thames – the sixteen foot wide pavement of the Blackwall Tunnel is perhaps the most impressive – but the risk of crime meant these were rarely popular.

Lastly, there were underground offices – a printing works under the Royal Exchange; a restaurant under St Paul's churchyard. And a whole host of light-fingered people had dreams of what lay under the Little Old Lady of Threadneedle Street – the Bank of England.

Charles Fort

The founder of Fortean phenomena is the only real-life American to feature in the Lestrade series.*

Charles Fort was born in Albany, New York in 1874 and hoped to be a naturalist. He travelled the world at the age of 18 and on his return married his childhood friend Anna Filing, who loved films and parakeets (and, one hopes, Charles Fort). He became a journalist but the death of a rich uncle in 1915 gave him the means to write whatever he liked full time.

His writings became more bizarre as he got older, claiming that Martians controlled life on earth and that an alien race lived under the ice of the South Pole. *The Book of the Damned* (1919) was an extensive dossier of phenomena for which science had no rational explanation.

In the mid '20s, Fort and Anna lived in London (which is where Lestrade met them) to study the arcane stuff housed in the library of the British Museum. Among the phenomena that Fort discussed were: ball lightning; spontaneous human combustion; showers of fish and frogs; poltergeist activity; levitation; UFOs; alien abduction and

---

* Suitable apologies to our friends in the colonies, but in Lestrade's day America was nowhere near being 'top nation' (we were) and there was no 'Special Relationship'. Live with it.

cryptozoology. Although all this won him a huge cult following, he once said, 'I believe nothing of my own that I have ever written.'

Does that mean that he didn't believe that line either? Hurts your head, doesn't it?

The Flying Squad
(Metropolitan Police, for the use of)

The Squad was responding to the increasingly mobile criminals of the 1920s. Each unit had a dozen officers commanded by an inspector and the drivers were given the honorary rank of Detective Constable. The Mobile Patrol Experiment of 1920 became the Flying Squad a year later and was part of CI, the Central CID.

Lestrade's protégé Inspector Walter Hambrook led the first unit, using a horse-drawn canvas van borrowed from the Great Western Railway with spy-holes cut in the side. By 1920, this was replaced by two Crossley tenders from the now demobilised Royal Flying Corps (which had been replaced by the RAF).

It was a small beginning and radio transmitters from the roof of Scotland Yard followed in 1923 using Morse Code. In many ways, it is a pity that the World's Second Greatest Detective was already retired, because the Crossleys with the radios had huge apparatus on their roofs which were known as bedsteads.

Oh, the endless jokes...

The Amateur of 221B

The accepted view is that Arthur Conan Doyle (qv) late of Edinburgh University Medical School, struggling to make a living as a doctor in Southsea, turned to writing to supplement his income.* He invented a doctor, Ormond Sacker, from Afghanistan and a philosopher and violin collector, Sherrinford Holmes and had them based at 221B Baker Street. By 1887, the pair had become John Watson and Sherlock Holmes and they appeared in *Beeton's Christmas Annual* in a story called *A Study in Scarlet*.

In 1891, the *Strand Magazine* commissioned more Holmes stories at £50 a pop. Wanting to carry on both medical research and to write serious historical novels (as opposed to tosh) Conan Doyle killed Holmes off in a desperate duel with the arch-fiend Professor Moriarty at the Reichenbach Falls in Switzerland. An outraged public demanded that the 'world's greatest detective' be brought back and Conan Doyle duly obliged in 1903 with stories in New York's *McClure's Magazine*.

A number of Scotland Yard detectives feature in the Holmes canon, but 'G. Lestrade', a 'little sallow, rat-faced, dark-eyed fellow' is 'the best of a bad bunch'. Holmes' arrogance knows no bounds and his exploits are still being

---

* Impossible to imagine this today, when doctors' salaries *far* outweigh authors' advances!

trotted out today (albeit in an updated form) on television (see **The Imposters**).

So, let's put the record straight once and for all. Sherlock Holmes was a cocaine addict with delusions. Believing that he had phenomenal powers of deduction, he set himself up in business as a 'consulting detective' at 221B Baker Street. His associate was John Watson, MD, late of the army medical service and his housekeeper was a Mrs Hudson, believed, like Conan Doyle, to be of the Scottish persuasion. Where, I hear you ask, does Conan Doyle fit into the story? He was a friend and colleague of Watson – who never seems to have had any patients, surgeries or medical work at all – and the pair thought it would be fun to write up Holmes' cases. How much artistic licence the pair used is anybody's guess but they foolishly lampooned the real police of the day, ridiculing the flatfeet of the Yard in particular. Hence the incorrect initial – 'G' – for Sholto Joseph Lestrade; it was a feeble attempt to avoid litigation.

Luckily for the good doctors, not to mention Holmes, Sholto Lestrade was not the vindictive type. He was perfectly happy to be known as the World's Second Greatest Detective, realising what a sad and tragic amateur Holmes was and that his ego was ever fragile. Incidentally, contrary to *The Return of Sherlock Holmes,* the doyen of 221B *did* die at Reichenbach, believing in his addicted confusion that the hapless tourist, Professor Moriarty, was John Watson, whom Holmes had come to hate with a passion.

In the fullness of time, Watson too became a murder victim but that, like so much else in the Lestrade canon, is another story.

The Imposters

Inspector Lestrade has been impersonated by a surprisingly large number of actors (and one actress!) because of the never-ending (and inexplicable) popularity of Sherlock Holmes. Wikipedia lists eighteen, but I suspect there are many more. IMDb currently has eighty-seven portrayals in film and television since 1931. I make no comment on the performances, if only because an actor is, by definition, in the strait-jacket of his lines. Since Conan Doyle called Lestrade 'a little sallow rat-faced, dark-eyed fellow' (in *A Study in Scarlet*) and a 'lean, ferret-like man, furtive and sly-looking' (in *The Boscombe Valley Mystery*), most casting directors have tried to oblige. Because Conan Doyle also referred to Lestrade as merely 'the best of a bad bunch' (ie of Scotland Yard detectives) screen and playwrights have followed suit, depicting Lestrade as various types of imbecile.

Below are listed the best known:

Dennis Hoey (Samuel Hyams) – since he was born in London in 1893, it's conceivable that he and Lestrade may have met! His son's biography *Elvis, Sherlock and Me* doesn't mention him however.

Frank Finlay – played the World's Second Greatest Detective twice, in what was actually the same story – *A Study in Terror* (1965) and *Murder By Decree* (1979)

Eddie Marsan – a recent arrival, Marsan was Lestrade in Guy Ritchie's *Sherlock Holmes* (2009) portraying the Inspector, for once, as perfectly competent and more than a little irritated by Holmes. 'Hurrah!' I hear you shout.

Ronald Lacey – played the Inspector in the 1983 version of *Hound of the Baskervilles* with Ian Richardson as Holmes. Spookily, he also played the Sholto brothers in Jeremy Brett's *The Sign of Four*.

Colin Jeavons – took on the role and was described by Granada Television's Michael Cox as 'the best Lestrade of his generation'. This was in *The Adventures of Sherlock Holmes* with Jeremy Brett as the amateur of Baker Street. Intriguingly, Jeavons also played the crime lord Professor Moriarty in *The Baker Street Boys* (1982).

Rupert Graves – has brought Lestrade into the twenty-first century in the BBC production *Sherlock*. As DI Greg Lestrade, Graves is a competent detective (Hurrah, again!) and cooperates with Holmes without being snide or grovelling as other versions have had to be.

Rob Brydon – watch this space! Ethan Cohen has grabbed Conan Doyle's characters by the scruff of their necks and the film is currently in post-production. From the IMDb information available, there seems to have been no historical adviser on the set. I, for one, am appalled!

Reginald Marsh – a special mention must be made of the late (and lovely) Reg Marsh, who played 'my' Inspector Lestrade in a playlet called *Exit Centre Stage* for local hospital radio in the Isle of Wight in the mid-'90s. He will always hold this first place, but if, Gentle Reader, you happen to be a TV exec or Hollywood producer, there's plenty of room for a follow-up or two. Please get in touch.

The Wit and Wisdom of Sholto Lestrade

The Inspector for whom no joke is too large or too small.

'Have you ever been hit by a jezail, Lestrade?'
'No, but I've been jostled by a Methodist.'

'Call me pernickety if you like …'
'Let's keep this formal shall we, Miss Dalrymple?'

'Good God, Lestrade, you could have given me a coronary.'
'Sorry, Doctor, there wasn't time.'

'Dervishes. They whirl, don't they?'
'Not when I've finished with them.'

'Are you a campanologist?'
'Politics aren't encouraged on the Force, sir.'

'Was that your clerk, Kent?'
'No, that was my clerk, Gable.'

'Anything Dew can do, I can do better. I can do anything better than Dew.'
'No, you can't.'
'Yes, I can; yes, I can.'

'Padraig Kellogg.'
'Who's he?'
'Ireland's only serial killer.'

'French on his mother's side.'
'Hmm. Nice to know there was *somebody* on his mother's side.'

'May I have his surname?'
'Belloc.'
'Well, of course, you aren't bound to tell me...'

'I'm not exactly cock-a-hoop over your breeches. Like many other things, they went out with Oscar Wilde.'

'No, I cannot accept it. I killed Dover.'
'Yes, I know you keeled over, but it doesn't matter. We only count falls in wrestling. Don't we?'

'Do you like me Widow Twanky?'
'Not just now; I'm on a case. And don't call me Widow Twanky.'

'Are you Newlove?'
'No, I've been here for months.'

'We aren't here to engage in semantics.'
Lestrade was glad to hear it. He'd had enough trouble with women, let alone Jewish ones.

'Arsehole Accrington, they called him – behind his back, of course.'

'Are you an aficionado, Mr Lestrade?'
'No; Church of England.'

'I've had a woman on the phone today.'
'That's not possible, surely?'

As you peruse the Lestrade series, Gentle Reader, feel free to add other gems here as you go – and mind how you go, of course!

Lightning Source UK Ltd.
Milton Keynes UK
UKHW041822090319
338831UK00001B/102/P